"Let me help

"And in exchange for my services, have dinner with me."

The devil must have murmured that same incantation in Eve's ear before she accepted the shiny apple, Molly thought. But would she be doomed if she took a teeny bite, a tiny bit of help from this man who was her competitor, her enemy?

Brandon Corral's offer was tempting. Very tempting. As were his lips…which smiled devilishly only a kiss away from her own.

Molly abruptly pivoted to stride away from him—and tripped. Brandon grasped her waist to steady her. It was a reflexive movement. But sexual tension exploded with the force of a lit gas main. Molly held his gaze, mesmerized, unable to move.

"You need my help," he whispered into her ear. "Why not just admit it?"

Dear Reader,

Happy New Year! I hope this year brings you all your heart desires…and I hope you enjoy the many books coming your way this year from Silhouette Special Edition!

January features an extraspecial THAT SPECIAL WOMAN!—Myrna Temte's *A Lawman for Kelly*. Deputy U.S. Marshal Steve Anderson is back (remember him in Myrna's *Room for Annie?*), and he's looking for love in Montana. Don't miss this warm, wonderful story!

Then travel to England this month with *Mistaken Bride*, by Brittany Young—a compelling Gothic story featuring two identical twins with very different personalities…. Or stay at home with *Live-In Mom* by Laurie Paige, a tender story about a little matchmaker determined to bring his stubborn dad to the altar with the right woman! And don't miss *Mr. Fix-It* by Jo Ann Algermissen. A man who is good around the house is great to find anytime during the year!

This month also brings you *The Lone Ranger*, the initial story in Sharon De Vita's winsome new series, SILVER CREEK COUNTY. Falling in love is all in a day's work in this charming Texas town. And watch for the first book by a wonderful writer who is new to Silhouette Special Edition—Neesa Hart. Her book, *Almost to the Altar*, is sure to win many new fans.

I hope this New Year shapes up to be the best year ever! Enjoy this book, and all the books to come!

Sincerely

Tara Gavin
Senior Editor

Please address questions and book requests to:
Silhouette Reader Service
U.S.: 3010 Walden Ave., P.O. Box 1325, Buffalo, NY 14269
Canadian: P.O. Box 609, Fort Erie, Ont. L2A 5X3

JO ANN ALGERMISSEN
MR. FIX-IT

SPECIAL EDITION®

Published by Silhouette Books
America's Publisher of Contemporary Romance

For Henry,
"Because You Love Me"

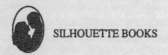 SILHOUETTE BOOKS

ISBN 0-373-24079-1

MR. FIX-IT

Copyright © 1997 by Jo Ann Algermissen

Books by Jo Ann Algermissen

Silhouette Special Edition

Silhouette Desire

Yours Truly

JO ANN ALGERMISSEN

is a prolific romance writer who smiles as she recalls selling her first three manuscripts *the same day*. Over the past fifteen years that number has grown to over forty. Married to her college sweetheart for thirty-two years, she practices the elements contained in every outstanding romance: love, commitment and happily-ever-after. She is also known to many of her readers by her maiden name, Anna Hudson.

Chapter One

"Got 'em!" John Winsome cheered as he placed the telephone receiver on its hook. "We start the plumbing grounds on the display houses within the next thirty days."

"Bayou Oaks?"

"And all of Norton's River Side subdivision, too!" John rubbed the palms of his hands together with glee. "So much for Corral Construction."

Molly watched her father strut between their two desks toward the map of Austin hanging on the wall as she silently calculated how many subcontract crews Winsome Plumbing would have to hire for the new job. Twin horizontal lines etched her brow. What John viewed as great news, she considered additional weight to his heavy work load.

His finger slashed an imaginary line east to west on the map with the same grit and determination with which Robert E. Lee must have defended the Mason-Dixon line during the War Between the States. South of the line small gray-and-yellow flags marked the subdivisions currently manned by Winsome's plumbers.

Without his having to ask for them, Molly opened her desk drawer and handed him several flag pins. "Do you still want me to do the takeoffs on the apartment project over by Barton Springs?"

"Is a forty-pound robin fat if he ain't long?" John teased.

Molly grinned. "Yeah . . . if he's skinny as a length of copper pipe and twenty feet tall."

"Sassy-mouthed kid." He chuckled his approval. "Of course I want to bid it. Corral got a toehold when he took over Shadrack's work in Wood Hollow. We can't let him outflank me by going circling around the city into Onion Creek."

"He is just another plumbing contractor, Dad."

"Didn't you hear the scuttlebutt? Corral bought out Bill Fontenout and Ron Gifford."

She hadn't heard. Although those two men were John's closest competitors, they were also her dad's poker-playing buddies. Among the three of them, they'd managed to do most of the residential plumbing work in Austin over the past twenty years.

Molly shook her head. "Guess they finally have the capital to develop those lake houses at Toledo Bend the three of you have talked about since I was a kid."

"That's what they said. My guess is they'll build retirement homes and give up the ghost." John poked some flags into the map, took a step backward and looked at his handiwork. "No fools like old fools. Can you picture me sitting by the lake with a cane fishing pole in my hand, wasting my life away?"

"No," she responded honestly. "But—"

He raised his hands to stop her tirade. "Don't start in on me about being the one who should have retired years ago. I know I'm the one with the bad ticker. But you read the report on my last checkup. The doc says I'm fit as a fiddle."

"With the bow slightly warped," Molly muttered, determined to have the last word.

John had the meaty physique of a professional linebacker, an occupation he'd aspired to in his youth. Gold trophies with a football player carrying a football attested to his athletic prowess.

His high-school trophies were prominently displayed in their office. But thirty years separated John from the playing field. Time and double helpings of fried chicken and mashed potatoes with redeye gravy had lowered his muscular pecs to his paunchy waistline.

Molly swiveled her chair around to face her computer and the blueprint spread out beside it. As far as her father's health was concerned, he thought he was invincible.

Only Molly knew better. The memory of him lying in the cardiac intensive care unit, close to death, was indelibly imprinted in her mind.

That had been five years ago, but she still felt pangs of guilt. If she'd been here to ease his load, maybe he would have worked shorter hours, slept without worrying about supervising the job sites and the office personnel. But no, she hadn't been here.

She'd been in Dallas—making the biggest mistake of her life—trying to squeeze her size-eleven feet into dainty size-five satin slippers. A modern-day Cinderella residing in a glitzy, glamorous purgatory.

Unwilling to waste time dwelling on past failures, she picked up the digital pen and traced the foundation line on the blueprint.

I'm here now. That's what counts.

Not that being here made an appreciable difference in her father's life-style, she silently admonished. John listened politely to her, then did as he damned well pleased. Her only consolation was knowing that she did lighten his load by doing the estimates, costing out the jobs and keeping a tight rein on the suppliers.

She wasn't the son he'd always wanted, nor could she ever hope to fill her father's shoes, but she could stand tall in her own boots.

Bent over the table, she surreptitiously watched her father pluck his straw hat from the hook beside the door.

"Going somewhere?"

"To celebrate underbidding Corral. Want to come along?"

The interoffice phone buzzed before she could reply. "Just a second. I told Yolanda to transfer your calls in here. This may be for you." She picked up the receiver. "Winsome Plumbing."

"Don't touch that hold button," a deep voice warned. "I've listened to enough of your country-western music to wear out the leather soles of my boots. Is John Winsome there?''

Tilting her head to one side, she motioned for her father to pick up the phone. "He is. Who should I tell him is calling?''

"Brandon Corral. Corral Plumbing."

Her blue eyes widened. She couldn't have been more surprised had he answered "The devil in blue jeans."

"Corral Plumbing,'' she repeated in a whisper as she held the telephone out toward her father. "Brandon Corral, to be specific.''

"Find out what he wants," John mouthed.

Accustomed to taking messages, Molly fibbed, "Mr. Winsome is on the other line. Is there something I can do for you?''

"Unless Mr. Winsome has authorized you to sell Winsome Plumbing to the highest bidder . . . no.''

Molly clamped her hand over the mouthpiece. "He wants to buy our company!''

Grinning, John took the phone. "Does six million strike you as a fair price?''

"Six million?'' Molly gasped. Dumbstruck by the inordinate figure, she tilted her chair back to see if her father was able to maintain a poker face. He was.

But Brandon Corral could not. She could hear his laughter loud and clear across the line.

"What's the matter, Corral? Can't you and your whiz kids compete fair and square? Gotta use your old man's money to buy up the competition?''

From the pink tinge creeping up her father's neck, Molly knew Brandon Corral wasn't meekly accepting her father's below-the-belt punches. He was delivering a few well-aimed jabs of his own.

"Today River Place," John blustered, "and tomorrow the Lakeview project at Hudson Bend. You'd better be careful of what you say, or next week my men will show your whiz kids up so badly your butt will be kicked out of Wood Hollow, too."

When John began rubbing his chest, Molly stood and reached for the phone. Nobody was going to verbally attack her father while she was around. He prevented her from snatching the phone by pivoting on one foot, until his back was to her. Frustrated, she balled her open hand into a fist.

"I don't give a rat's patoot what kind of arrangement you made with Gifford and Fontenout. I may be old, but I'm not senile. The day I let Corral Plumbing put their brand on my butt is the same day the toe of my boot will be firmly planted on your backside." With that proclamation of war, John banged down the phone. "Don't accept any more of his calls... ever!"

"What'd he say, Dad?"

"He insinuated that I'd better sell out before I go bankrupt trying to underbid him." John plowed his fingers through his sparse gray hair. "Then he implied that I must have lost my ever-lovin' mind to submit such low bids to a general contractor. He practically called me a crazy old coot!"

Like father like daughter, Molly felt a head of steam rising from beneath her shirt collar. It wasn't necessary to look in the mirror to know her neck and face had turned beet red, too.

"I checked the calculations twice on the computer. Unless there is a dramatic price hike in the cost of PVC and copper, we'll make our usual profit."

Molly sounded confident, but her stomach did a somersault. The final analysis the computer spit out was only as accurate as the information the operator typed into the data base. Feverishly she began sorting through the stack of reports on her desk until she found the folder marked Bayou Oaks.

Lord have mercy, she prayed, don't let me be the weak link in the chain of command.

"Here are the figures." Molly held out the folder. "You're welcome to go over them if you doubt my accuracy."

She was so intent on defending her cost estimates that she was startled when the telephone buzzed. Certain Mr. Corral had taken umbrage at having the phone slammed down in his ear, she grabbed the receiver before her father could reach it. She had a few choice words of her own to say to the man.

"City morgue. You stab 'em, we slab 'em," she quipped, her humor as dark as her thoughts.

"The morgue doesn't play country-western while calls are being transferred. Let me speak to Winsome again," Brand ordered.

"Over my dead body, Mr. Corral."

"Who is this?"

"Molly Winsome, estimator *extraordinaire*, vice president to you."

"Winsome's wife?"

"Daughter." Eager to make him apologize for the nasty swipes he'd taken at John, she added, "But don't worry...senility isn't hereditary or contagious."

"Do you have any influence on your father's decisions?"

Molly clenched her teeth. The man had no shame! "That 'crazy old coot'?" she asked, quoting him. "You aren't the only one who doesn't hear a word I say."

"What do you do at Winsome Plumbing other than antagonize the people who call your father?"

"Peer into my crystal ball and come up with magical numbers. I write them on scraps of paper, and I mail them to general contractors and call them *bids*."

"Not 'magical' numbers. Ungodly low numbers," Brandon corrected, deeming her bids outrageously insufficient.

"Do you think maybe I should have bought the expensive crystal ball that came with eights, nines and tens in it?"

"Lady, you honestly don't want to know what I'm thinking."

Like her father, Molly had no intention of continuing to swap insults with Brandon Corral. They'd underbid him, John had refused to sell out and Corral was being a sore loser.

"You don't have to tell me what's on your mind." Molly paused for dramatic effect. "I can read your mind. Wait a second. My crystal ball is a little fuzzy, but you're beginning to come in loud and clear."

Although tempted to bang the receiver on the edge of the desk before slamming it down, she decided she wouldn't give Corral the satisfaction of knowing she'd hung up on him.

Music was supposed to soothe the savage beast, wasn't it? Let him listen to Garth Brooks's rendition of "Friends in Low Places"!

Ever so gently, Molly put the receiver next to the radio and motioned for her father to precede her out of the office. Far, far sweeter than losing control of her temper was the delicious prospect of Brandon Corral wasting his precious time waiting for a crystal-ball report.

"We'll file that unpleasant conversation under the heading 'Win Some, Lose Some, Some Get Rained Out—and Some Get Put on Hold'!" she mouthed.

Brandon waited several seconds, unsure what to make of Winsome's daughter. In the reports he'd accumulated on Winsome Plumbing, she'd been cited as the brains behind the business. John handled the crews; she ran the office. Brandon would hire her quicker than a wink if she were anyone other than Winsome's daughter.

Leaning back in his chair, he opened the file folder labeled "Winsome Plumbing." Before this provocative phone conversation, he'd only been interested in the facts and figures he'd used to make a fair offer for their company. He'd merely glanced at the color photo accompanying a lengthy newspaper article. The caption read: "Contractor Celebrates Fortieth Year in Business." Now he examined the picture.

Dressed in faded jeans, a blue chambray shirt and high-heeled boots, Molly Winsome stood eye to eye with her father, who had to be at least six feet tall without his boots. But that's where the similarities ended.

John's middle-age spread hung over his wide belt buckle; Molly's figure was rounded, in all the right places. The father's eyes were dark; his daughter's eyes were light. He had a short, military haircut; Molly's reddish brown hair was French-braided and as thick as a man's upper arm.

Brand cradled the telephone receiver between his clean-shaven jaw and his shoulder. He focused his attention on the woman in the picture. Although attractive, he wouldn't classify Molly as cute, at least not in the Dallas Cowgirl sense of the word.

He held the picture closer, studying her grin, the slight tilt of her nose. Briefly narrowing his eyes, he stared at her. He imagined himself unplaiting her braid, wrapping those loosened thick strands of hair around his wrist. Tall as she was, he wouldn't have to bend in half to kiss her provocative lips. One arm could easily wrap around her slender waist. From the womanly curve of her hips, he knew her backside would fit nicely into his hands. He blinked to dispel the erotic sensation of having Molly Winsome held tightly against him.

Damned attractive, he amended, feeling male hormones surge through him. There was something about her that made him certain Molly Winsome was a woman a man couldn't easily forget.

What was it? Pride and self-confidence, mixed with...vulnerability? Those barely hidden qualities intrigued him as much as her claim of owning a crystal ball.

By the time the seconds had strung into minutes and the rowdy Brooks chorus had changed to the mournful wailing of a brokenhearted cowgirl, Brandon's patience had worn thin.

"Well?" he demanded. "What does your crystal ball tell you I am thinking?"

"'Blue-hoo-hoo, and cryin' over you-hoo-hoo...'"

"Hello? Ms. Winsome?" He stopped himself from asking inanely, "Are you there?"

"Very subtle," he commented, disconnecting the line. "Her crystal ball says I'm the village idiot."

A begrudging smile curved his mouth upward. After one last look he dropped her photo back into the folder. Having second thoughts, he placed the picture squarely in the center of his desk and shoved the folder aside.

"Ms. Molly," he whispered, his Southern accent as sweet and rich as a slice of pecan pie, "silence doesn't qualify you as victorious. That honor will be mine."

"You handled Brandon Corral well, Daughter," John praised. The door of his battered yellow pickup truck groaned in protest as he opened it. He slid across the tattered seat. "I would have lost my temper again if I'd spoken to him."

"He who loses his temper loses. Isn't that one of the many principles of business you taught me?"

"Yeah...along with don't ask anybody to do anything you wouldn't do yourself."

"You didn't ask me to talk to Mr. Corral. I made that decision." She grinned and winked at her dad. The slightest praise from her father had her feeling ten feet tall—and not minding it. "Thanks for the compliment, though."

John put his key in the ignition, but delayed starting the engine. Molly shut the door for him.

"I don't know what it is about Brandon Corral that riles me. He's my competitor, but so what? For years my two strongest competitors have also been my two best friends."

"Does it bother you that they sold out to Corral?"

"A little." John curled one arm over the steering wheel and cocked his other elbow out the window. "Makes me feel old."

Molly barely heard what he'd muttered. "Old? You? Come on, Dad. You and I both know you'll pipe another ten thousand houses before you voluntarily call it quits."

"What if I don't?" John frowned. "What would you do if I dragged my fishin' pole out of the garage and trotted off to Toledo Bend with my buddies?"

The preposterous idea brought laughter bubbling through Molly's lips. "Am I talking to the same man who told me his ego was firmly attached to his billfold? That any day Winsome didn't make money would be the day he'd feel he could stand tall and still be able to walk under a closed door?" She lightly punched his arm. "I worry about you working too hard, Dad, not putting a Gone Fishing sign on the door."

John's grimace turned into a thin line of distaste. "I figure Corral is in his early thirties, but his company completes more houses in a week than we do in a month. Guess having a leg up when you start out helps, huh?"

"A leg up?"

"Sure. Brandon Corral is Jake Corral's grandson."

"The guy who advertises cars on television?"

"The same geezer who owns half the dealerships in Austin, Houston and San Antonio. Brandon is a rich man's kid. Why do you think I put such an exorbitant price on Winsome Plumbing?"

Molly shrugged. "Your company is worth double that amount to you."

"Maybe it is, come to think of it." He reached out and ruffled his daughter's bangs. "Don't you worry your pretty little head, Coppertop. I'm not going to sell out to Brandon Corral for any amount of money. In fact, I think I'll head on over to Wood Hollow and see if I can take Cervelle's superintendent out to lunch. Who knows, maybe I can make good on my threat to get Ron and Bill's houses away from Brandon's whiz kids. See you later."

Over the roar of the engine, Molly shouted, "Don't be late for dinner."

"Call Kate and tell her not to take mine out of the freezer and microwave it until I get there," he teased, waving as he backed out of the parking lot.

Laughing at his standard joke about her mother's lack of culinary skills, Molly strode back into the warehouse. She paused for a second, visually making a rough estimate of how many lengths of copper pipe they had in inventory. Not enough, she noted, calculating how much they'd need to top out the six houses John had mentioned would soon be ready.

To keep inventory costs down, she ordered only what they needed.

"Must be nice to have a 'leg up' and not have to worry about bothersome details—like how to pay a supplier within thirty days," she murmured, momentarily envious of Brandon Corral's capital.

She quickly changed her mind. She'd had all the advantages of wealth...and the disadvantages, which no one talked about.

She'd blindly gone into marriage thinking love was the sole element necessary for a successful marriage.

No one had told her she'd have to drastically change to fit the image of a wife. Things she'd considered a waste of time—such as window-shopping, going to the beauty salon and the exercise gym—he'd considered necessary.

No one had taught her how to manage a large household staff. Foolishly, she'd tried to be friendly and helpful. If there was work to be done, she couldn't sit idle and wait for another person to do it. She'd rolled up the sleeves on her designer dress and pitched right in. Her husband had been appalled the day he'd come home and found her under the sink, replacing a leaky pipe.

No one had told her she'd wake up each morning wondering how she'd pass the day until her husband came home. Or that she'd be bored stiff. It had taken three years for her to realize she detested the type of shallow, sophisticated woman her husband wanted.

Molly crossed the hallway between the warehouse and her office, glad to get back to work. Here she was useful. Responsible. Productive. Competent. Here she felt an immense sense of accomplishment when jobs were completed. She wouldn't trade those feelings for any amount of cash reserve.

* * *

"I'm in the northwest end of Austin, checking out the progress on the model homes, Mrs. O'Connor," Brandon said to his office assistant via cellular phone. "Any messages?"

"Your grandfather called. Nothing urgent."

"I'll get back to him later." Brandon equated a call from Lincoln to a broken water main. "I won't make it back to the office before five o'clock. See you in the morning. Bye."

The bright rays of the setting September sun momentarily blinded Brandon as he drove into the Wood Hollow subdivision. He shielded his eyes with his hand while lowering the sun visor.

Typical fall Texas weather, he thought, switching off his windshield wipers. Rain east of I-35 and clear skies in the Hill Country.

He parked his Suburban at the curb and glanced over his shoulder at the foreboding clouds rolling in from the north. Normally the job site would have been a beehive of activity. Today, though, his men had been smart enough to pack up their equipment early. Ominous clouds filled with crackling bolts of lightning were a danger that no seasoned construction worker easily dismissed.

Slowly he lifted his foot off the brake and eased forward, leaning across the passenger's seat to view the work in progress. Wooden skeletons of five two-story houses, in various stages of completion, stood empty. Weather permitting, his top-out crews would have pipe strung from one end of the buildings to the other by the end of the week.

On schedule, he surmised, smiling at the thought. Winsome could make wild threats about the general contractor kicking Corral Plumbing off the job, but that wouldn't happen as long as they continued doing quality work in a timely manner.

Unable to resist the urge to check out his competitor's work, Brandon wound through the maze of streets to the opposite end of the subdivision, where Nationwide Homes had given the contract to Winsome Plumbing. Much as he wanted to find fault, Brandon noticed the same number of houses nearing completion.

He also noticed Winsome's dilapidated truck pulled up beside the model home. Raising the sun visor, he quickly scanned the brick exterior of the completed house.

"What the hell," he murmured. There, perched on the steep slope of a three-story roof, was old man Winsome. He held a hammer in one hand and a roof flashing in the other.

Brandon slammed on his brakes and climbed out of his truck. A gust of wind plastered his white shirt and gray slacks against his lean frame. Swirls of dust permeated the humid air.

"Get down from there!" he shouted to John.

"Roofer forgot this flashing." He pointed toward the white plastic pipe rising through the shingles. "Got to get it on this pipe or the rain will flood the house."

"Get down!" Damned fool! What was he trying to do? Get himself killed?

Suddenly another gust, at least fifty miles an hour, whipped across the roof. The shingles the older man had pried loose took flight, striking him in the face.

Brandon stood helplessly on the ground as he watched Winsome lose his balance. In what seemed like slow motion, he saw the man's arms flail. Winsome dropped the hammer, and gravity pulled it away, sending it skittering along the shingles until it lodged in the storm gutter. He was caught off-balance, and his footing slipped. He grabbed for the pipe, but missed.

"Noooooo!" John screamed.

Or was it Brandon who screamed?

Brandon charged toward the house. His head bobbed upward, then downward, as he leaped over mounds of discarded lumber strewn in the front of the lot, trying to keep an eye on John.

Mercifully, he didn't see the older man hit the ground. Scant seconds later, Brandon dropped to his knees beside Winsome's crumpled body.

Chapter Two

Brandon's eyes traveled over his fiercest competitor. The rough shingles had scraped one side of John Winsome's face and both his hands. His leg appeared bent back at an odd angle. Panic welled up inside Brandon, but his hands moved quickly. He opened the top button of John's plaid shirt and felt for a pulse.

He was alive and breathing. Thank God!

"You're going to be okay, Mr. Winsome." Brandon didn't know if he was reassuring the unconscious man or himself, but he did know that he needed to get help. *Immediately.* "I'll be right back!"

His heart pounded in his ears, louder than the wind howling through the open studs in the surrounding buildings. He raced back to his truck, grabbed the cellular phone and dialed the nationwide three-digit emergency number. His hand shook as he held the receiver to his ear.

"Nine-one-one Emergency."

"There's been an accident at 552 Prairie Creek in the new Wood Hollow subdivision off Route 518. A man has fallen from a third-story roof."

The operator repeated the address. "Please hold while I dispatch an ambulance."

Brandon took several deep breaths in an effort to calm his nerves. He strained to see through the debris obstructing his view of John. At this stage of building, the piles of rubbish should have been cleared away! The feeling of helplessness, of not knowing what to do, overwhelmed him.

When the operator began asking questions, Brandon felt completely inadequate, totally unprepared for a medical emergency. Hell, he didn't even have a first-aid kit in his truck. There was one at the construction-site trailer, but he couldn't leave John to retrieve it.

"Do you have a blanket in your vehicle or a coat?"

"Yes! There's a stadium blanket in the truck."

As he listened to the operator's instructions on what to do to prevent shock, he scrambled over the console and struggled to reach into the back compartment where he stored the blanket. Suddenly it occurred to him that he was talking on the cellular phone—there was no telephone wire to keep him tied to the dashboard. Feeling foolish, he lunged over the back seat and grabbed the blanket.

"Got it."

"Good. Cover him up, but don't—ove—hi— The ambul—way."

Damn! This was a helluva time for the reception to fade.

"You're breaking up," he yelled. Static and wind were the only replies. A swearword straight from the pages of a seasoned construction laborer's handbook hissed between his lips.

Seconds that seemed like hours later, Brandon lowered the woolen blanket over John. He hadn't moved an inch.

"Mr. Winsome? John? Can you hear me?" On his hands and knees, Brandon hunkered over Winsome to protect him from the force of the wind. Spatters of rain pelted his broad shoulders. "An ambulance is on its way. Hang on, old-timer."

He thought he heard a groan, but it could have been the wind.

"Don't you die, Winsome!" Brandon was unsure John understood what he was saying to him. Yet he was determined to give the old man the will to live. "So help me, if you croak I'll take over every house you have under contract!"

Brandon felt the man's fingers wad the front of his shirt and heard, "Kick...your...butt, whiz kid."

From a distance Brandon caught the wail of a siren. Come on, dammit! He silently urged the driver to drive faster. The blue pallor of John's lips scared him.

Brandon felt the fingers clutching his shirt relax their hold. Refusing to let them fall limply on John's chest, he clasped the man's hand and challenged, "When?"

"Later," John whispered, his voice weaker than the mewl of a newborn kitten.

For an instant Brandon saw the dark gleam of anger glistening in John's eyes. His heart plummeted to his toes when seconds later all he could see was the whites of the man's eyes.

"C'mon. Fight! Hang in there. Dammit, I won't let you die."

His mind searched for another scrap of information he could wield against John. He was losing him. Brandon gripped his knuckles hard enough to make a strong man wince. He'd do anything, say anything, to get a response from John.

"What about Molly? Are you going to let a woman take over a man's job? Winsome Plumbing will go bankrupt in no time flat!"

He had believed John to be unconscious, maybe dead. His eyes widened in amazement as the old man's lips twitched, then curved into a feeble smile.

"She'll sell out," Brandon goaded.

John barely shook his head.

"We both know a woman can't run a construction business." He heard a vehicle racing up the street, siren blaring, but he was afraid to take his eyes off John. "And when she sells, I'll be there."

"Okay, mister," the medic said, placing his hand on Brandon's shoulder. "You did fine. We'll take over now."

"His name is John Winsome. He's been drifting in and out of consciousness." Reluctant to let go of John's hand, Brandon dropped back on his haunches.

For several moments he watched as the medic took John's pulse and blood pressure. Forced to relinquish his grasp when the medic put a stethoscope to John's chest, Brandon rose to his feet. His knees felt weak and shaky. An emotional knot wedged in his throat as he watched the medic's face. Whatever he'd heard wasn't good.

"Get that stretcher over here—fast," the medic yelled over his shoulder. He removed a radio from his belt and began feeding vital statistics back to the hospital while his co-workers prepared to move John onto the stretcher. "Compound fracture of the femur, broken ribs, possible concussion."

Brandon shifted from one foot to the other, feeling useless, biting back his fear by clenching his teeth. The moan he heard as they lifted John onto the stretcher sliced through him.

"You a relative?" the medic asked as he hurriedly packed away his diagnostic equipment and followed the men carrying the stretcher.

"No." Brandon jogged alongside the medic until they reached the ambulance.

"Friend?"

He parted his lips to automatically respond no. He wasn't John Winsome's friend. Until the accident, he'd had several choice names for John Winsome, none of which came within yards of being friendship. John's company blocked his goal of becoming the largest residential plumbing contractor in Austin. They were business rivals, staunch competitors ... enemies.

And yet, with the imprint of John's calluses lingering on his palm, he couldn't deny friendship. Had this life-and-death crisis formed an undeniable bond between them?

"Yes," Brandon replied, answering the medic and his own silent probe. "Where are you taking him?"

"Seaton Hospital."

"Is there anything I can do?"

The ambulance rolled forward as the driver said, "We'll take care of him. The hospital will notify Mr. Winsome's family."

The orange-and-white ambulance quickly disappeared from sight. Brandon disliked the idea of John's family being notified by strangers. He also hated like the devil to be the bearer of bad news to Molly Winsome. He'd promised to have the last word when she'd left him dangling on the telephone, but telling Molly her father was in critical condition after falling off a roof wasn't what he'd had in mind.

He could deal with women in a business setting, but the thought of handling an emotional scene chilled him to the bone. Unlike a man, a woman fell apart in a crisis. Molly would probably get hysterical and cry. On the few occasions that a woman had wept and clung to him, he'd felt totally flummoxed. Having been raised by his grandfather while his parents had traipsed around the globe collecting antiques had its disadvantages. Neither his nanny nor the maids had shed tears in his presence.

What would he do if Molly heard the bad news and started blubbering?

Brandon scowled, feeling like a coward.

Should he or shouldn't he take the responsibility for contacting Molly?

Brandon scorned indecisiveness, considering it a blueprint for failure. He relied on his gut instincts to make split-second decisions. And yet here he was, standing on the curb of a deserted subdivision during a cloudburst, dithering away valuable time.

Do something. Anything!

He swiped the rivulets of rain off his face with the sleeve of his shirt. He turned, studying the roof of the model home. John Winsome had risked his life to put a flashing on that piece of naked pipe. Like water pouring into a sink with no stopper, the rain had to be coursing through the hole in the roof, drenching the insulation and drywall.

Spurred by the costly consequences of rain damage to John's building, Brandon jogged to the back of his truck and retrieved his tool belt. He buckled it to his waist as he raced to the ladder leaning against the side of the building. Certain the shingles would be treacherously slippery, he kicked off his leather-soled boots and shed his socks. He'd need every bit of traction his bare feet would give him.

With each rung he climbed, his confidence began to restore itself. Carefully he stepped from the top rung of the ladder to the roof. He picked up the flashing John had dropped. Inch by laborious inch, on hands and knees, he crawled toward his objective. His fingers and toenails clung to each crevice in the roof. Every ounce of concentration and willpower he possessed was focused on challenging the wind and rain's force. When he reached the pipe, he slid on the flashing, then secured it by hammering in several nails, until the water no longer drained into the house.

Relieved to have accomplished the task John had begun, he took a deep breath and began his dangerous trek back to the ladder. He wasn't infallible. He'd be the first to admit that he'd been unqualified to handle John's medical emergency. And he would probably have bungled comforting Molly, too. But by damned, there wasn't any builder in Austin—hell, maybe in all of Texas—who could top him when it came to building a house. He could— Ooops!

Brandon's thoughts were abruptly interrupted by his knees skidding southward. The rough surface of the shingles pulled his shirt up and raked across his belly. As his fingers clambered to find a hold, he had the same sensation he'd had as a kid when he'd tried to go up a down escalator.

His feet rammed into the storm gutter, stopping his fall.

"Damn! What a ride!"

And then the rivets holding the gutter to the frame of the house began to pop loose. The gutter struck the ladder and knocked it to the ground. Gritting his teeth, Brandon felt gravity pulling at his legs. His heart pounded frantically. His fingernails sounded as though they were scratching a chalkboard as he clawed the shingles. Unless he could break his momentum, within seconds he'd be flat on his back where John had been, with one major difference. There was no one around to pick up the pieces!

Molly's mother gripped her hand as though it were a lifeline in a stormy sea.

"He's going to be okay, Mom," Molly reassured her for the tenth time in as many minutes. "Dr. Aspenwald said—"

"I don't give a hoot what the doctor said. You can't make me believe they're keeping John here with a broken leg, a few cracked ribs and a mild concussion. You mark my word, he's had another heart attack. They're keeping the bad news until last." Kate lowered her voice to a fierce whisper. "Your dad hates hospitals."

Molly worried her bottom lip. Her mother had visibly aged during the past hour. Stress had carved deep lines across her forehead and cheeks, where previously there had been only slight wrinkles. Kate's short, curly hair practically stood on end from her nervously plowing her fingers through it. She'd chewed off what little lipstick she normally wore.

"What's keeping them so long?" Kate demanded. "I could have taped his ribs and put both his legs in a cast by now."

Molly glanced from her mother's drawn face to the two empty beds in the room. "Why don't you lie down and rest until—"

"No! I know how hospitals work. They aren't wheeling me off for a battery of expensive tests!"

Prolonged tension caused Molly to chuckle and shake her head. "Mother..."

"Don't laugh and shake your head at me. That's exactly what happened on one of my programs. Poor Maude. She made the mistake of lying down to take a catnap while tests were being run on her husband. The next thing she knew she woke up in the recovery room...with one breast missing!"

"Mother, that only happens on the soaps," Molly protested mildly. When she saw her mother dabbing at her eyes with a tissue, she regretted her disparaging remark. "Aw, Mom, don't cry. It will upset Dad if he sees you crying."

Kate sniffed. "I know I'm overreacting, but you and John are all I've got. Your dad could have been killed. What was he doing up on that roof to begin with?''

That was a question Molly had repeatedly asked herself during the drive to the hospital. When she'd been told the address where the accident had occurred, she'd been completely stymied.

"I don't know. The model house in Wood Hollow is finished."

"If that young man—what's his name?"

"Corral." Molly's dark blue eyes narrowed as she speculated on why he'd been at the site of the accident. "Brandon Corral."

Her own imagination took flight while her mother continued to praise the man who'd rescued her father. Was it pure coincidence that brought the two men together after they'd had words on the telephone? During a howling storm blowing in off the Gulf? She doubted it.

Somehow, Corral had known her father would be out there. And he'd lured John onto the roof. They'd argued. When John had refused to sell his company, Corral had...what? Had they gotten into a fistfight? In spite of his age, John was a big man, a man who could take care of himself. Maybe Corral had waited until John had his back turned and deliberately pushed him from behind. Then what? He'd called an ambulance to make it look like an accident?

Prejudiced as she was against Brandon Corral, that scenario didn't make sense. But then again, maybe it did. Maybe in a moment of remorse he'd placed the call and covered John with a blanket. Or maybe he'd panicked and thrown the blanket over John to conceal the body.

Right now he was probably at a bar, soaking up some suds, dreaming up a cock-and-bull story while he waited for the cops to come and arrest him. If her suspicions held a grain of truth, when her father verified them she'd go with the police and request the pleasure of personally handcuffing Mr. Brandon Corral . . . to the bumper of the squad car!

"Don't you think you should do that?" Kate inquired, placing the stadium blanket the nurse had given them in Molly's lap. "Molly? Are you listening to me?"

Molly glanced down at the bold red plaid woolen blanket. "What?"

"Never mind. Just return the blanket to Mr. Corral." Kate jumped to her feet and briskly strode toward the door. "Here they come with your dad."

"He's been given a sedative," the nurse informed Kate. "Dr. Aspenwald will speak to you in the hallway while we get your husband into bed."

Molly took one look at her father's battered face, bandaged hands and the hip-to-toe cast on his leg and decided chaining Brandon Corral to a police car and dragging him down every street in Austin was too light a punishment.

He should be horsewhipped at each intersection, she added silently.

While Kate talked to the doctor, Molly twisted the blanket between her hands as she waited for the nurse and orderlies to get her father settled. Once they'd tucked him in, she dropped the blanket and moved to his bedside.

"Dad," she murmured, gently taking his bandaged hand and holding it beside her face. As much as it hurt to see him in such a pitiful condition, she was glad she was here. "I love you."

His eyelids fluttered open. Slowly, with supreme effort, he mouthed, "Company... don't sell."

A salty lump lodged in her throat, which made it impossible to speak. She swallowed hard. Tears welled in her eyes. She blinked rapidly to control them.

Damn your stinking hide, Brandon Corral, she condemned silently.

"Don't worry," she soothed, her voice strained and husky. "I'll take care of everything."

"Get Corral... to helllll—"

Molly tenderly placed her finger across her father's lips before he could finish. "I'll make him pay for what he did to you, Dad."

John struggled to communicate, then gave up and allowed the drugs he'd been given to do their job.

"He's asleep?" Kate whispered, putting one arm across her daughter's shoulders.

Molly nodded. She felt her mother drawing her away from the bedside.

When they were out of earshot Kate asked, "Did he say anything?"

"Yeah. He said..." She paused long enough to tactfully alter the truth. Like her father, she protected her mother from unnecessary anxiety. "He loves us."

"He's such a precious man. The doctor says John's lucky one of his broken ribs didn't pierce a lung." A long shudder passed through Kate's slender body. "He could have died out there if he'd been alone."

In an effort to cheer up her mother, Molly said, "He's too ornery to die."

Kate smiled weakly and squeezed Molly's shoulder. "Yeah, well, he's also too old to be climbing on rooftops. While he's stuck here, we're going to have a heart-to-heart talk about Winsome Plumbing."

"Don't worry Dad about the business. I promised him I'd take care of everything." Molly received an all-too-familiar look of complete bafflement from her mother. Kate had never been able to comprehend why her daughter loved the building trades. Rather than listen to the you-ought-to-get-married-again-and-provide-me-with-grandchildren lecture that always followed that "look," she asked, "How long does the doctor think he'll have to be hospitalized?"

"Who knows? They're concerned about his ribs. A sneeze could jar them and cause more damage. They may have to put his leg in traction." She crossed to the chair, picked up the blanket and handed it to Molly. "I've made arrangements to stay here overnight to keep an eye on him. I want you to take this to that nice Mr. Corral and thank him for helping your father."

"Mother," Molly protested. "I'm not going to—"

"Don't argue with me, Daughter. There is no reason for both of us to stay here. If you're going to step into your father's boots, you're going to need a good night's rest. Tomorrow you can take care of returning the blanket, first thing."

"But—"

"No buts!" Kate refuted firmly. "Your father would want you to do what I asked."

Molly's mouth opened automatically, then clamped shut. She recognized that bull-terrier stubborn streak emanating from her mother's blue eyes. There was no reasoning with her when she was upset.

"Okay," she acquiesced.

"Don't pull that 'Okay' and then go off and do as you please. Okay what?"

"Just...okay. I'll do it," she fibbed to pacify her mother.

"Promise?"

They both turned when John groaned and shifted restlessly. Molly started to go see if she could help him, but her mother caught her arm. This wasn't the time or place for lengthy explanations. "Promise," she conceded.

Within minutes, Kate shooed her out of the hospital room with a militant "I'll take good care of your dad. You keep your promise."

"That nice Mr. Corral," Molly muttered moments later, mimicking her mother, as she flung the blanket into the front seat of her truck. "I'll give him the thanks he deserves!"

She needed to stop by the office to check the subcontractor's work list—which crews worked where—and contact the general contractor's job superintendents. It was essential to establish an air of "business as usual."

But first, she was going to drive by Wood Hollow and search for incriminating evidence.

A full moon shone brightly, casting iridescent light across the Texas State Capitol building. Normally

when she drove on Capitol Hills Highway she felt a
sense of Texas pride as she glanced through the granite hills at the skyline. Tonight her attention focused
on outmaneuvering the other drivers. Austin earned
its reputation for down-home hospitality—and for
those charming people turning into speed demons
when they climbed into their cars.

Ten minutes later she swung into the partially developed subdivision. She wove through the empty
streets until she reached the model house. A Suburban she didn't recognize was parked at the curb.

Must have had engine trouble, she thought dismis-
sively as she stepped from her truck. Whoever owned
it would be lucky if it wasn't stripped or stolen by
morning.

She pulled a flashlight from under the seat.

"Hey! You!"

The booming voice echoed from out of nowhere.
Molly felt a shiver run up her spine. A woman alone
in a deserted area wasn't safe. In the past they'd had
trouble with illegal aliens spending nights in the
buildings. She flashed a beam of light across the exterior walls.

"Whoever you are, you'd better find another place
to sleep. The night watchman will be here shortly,"
she lied. The general contractor had refused her sug-
gestion to hire a night watchman, but she didn't want
this man to know it. She swept the beam through the
windows. "He's only a block or two away."

"I'm up here, lady. On the roof."

Molly raised the flashlight. The beam traced a path
up the brick, across the gutter hanging askew,
searching until it landed on the man hunkered beside

the chimney. Any hope she'd had of finding evidence against Corral began to fade.

"What are you doing up there?"

"Bird-watching," Brandon replied snidely. Soaked to the skin, scraped and bruised, not to mention feeling like a complete fool, he was in no mood for chit-chat.

"Oh yeah?" His smart-aleck answer convinced Molly the man was up to no good. Only a raving lunatic would sit on a roof during a rainstorm. In her most authoritarian voice, she yelled, "Get down off the roof. This is private property. I want to see some identification."

"Don't you think I would if I could? The ladder fell." To hide his embarrassment, he added cockily, "I would have played Superman and flown down, but I left my costume in a phone booth."

For a man in a precarious situation, he sure had a smart mouth, Molly surmised. She spotted the ladder, on its side, mired in the mud beside the building, before she put the flashlight on the ground. She'd need both hands to position it against the front of the house.

"Wait." Brandon straightened, regretting his brash reply. "You can't leave me stranded!"

Molly smiled. In the pitch-blackness he couldn't see that she was about to save him. The waterlogged wooden ladder weighed a ton. Silently groaning, she had to give a mighty heave to extract it.

"Just sit tight." She panted from exertion. "I'll have you down from there in a jiffy.

"Good thing I'm not a pint-size weakling," she muttered. "Your typical Southern belle with a size-five shoe couldn't have lifted this."

Brandon heard her, but he couldn't figure out what shoe size had to do with ladders. "What did you say?"

"Nothing." Old habits die hard, she thought. It had been months since she'd compared herself with the petite fashion-plate woman her ex-husband had married. She pivoted the ladder into an upright position, then leaned it against the house. "Try not to break your neck getting down."

Standing beside the ladder, Molly raised the flashlight to light the rungs for him. Noticing the wide leather carpenter's belt that settled low on his trim hips, she assumed he must be one of the men her father had recently hired. Beneath the damp cotton fabric straining across his back, she could see the play of muscles. Her eyes dropped to the backside of his gray slacks, then to his long powerful legs.

Unconscious of doing it, she crossed her arms over her chest protectively as her heart skipped a beat.

"Why were you up there?" she asked when he'd dismounted from the ladder.

"The roofer forgot a flashing. Rain was pouring through it until I fixed it." He raked his fingers through his damp hair, then blocked the beam of light from his eyes. "Would you mind?"

She did, but she lowered the flashlight. This carpenter had to be one of the best-looking men she'd ever laid eyes on. He had a tanned, olive complexion; dark, straight hair; and brown eyes that belonged in a bedroom.

Very handsome and very, very sexy, she thought, remembering the lengthy view she'd had of his back- side. And tall. Without her boots she stood close to six feet tall. Barefoot, he towered over her a good six inches.

Barefoot?

She pointed her flashlight from his bare chest to his bare toes. "Do you always work nude?"

"Only at night."

That grin of his had the power to turn the strong muscles of her thighs to putty. Molly felt her cheeks tingle with warmth. She'd deserved that. Whatever in the world had made her ask such a provocative ques- tion of a complete stranger? Her only saving grace was knowing he couldn't see her blush. She scanned the ground with the light.

"There they are," Brandon said, pointing to his boots. "Hold the light steady. I don't need to round out a perfectly miserable evening by puncturing my foot with a nail."

"Guess we owe you some overtime on your pay- check," Molly suddenly said.

"We?"

"Winsome Plumbing. I'm John's daughter, Molly."

The woman with the crystal ball and the toe- tapping country music? He hadn't recognized her from the picture in his file.

The photograph hadn't done her justice. He'd thought her attractive, damned attractive, but in real life she was stunningly beautiful.

Brandon rammed his bare foot into his boot; his clammy socks were a lost cause. Careful to avoid putting his other foot in his mouth, he grunted a deferential "Yes, ma'am."

Now that their boss-employee relationship was established and Molly was certain he wasn't a vandal, she felt more at ease. She glanced toward the chimney. "John was pushed off that roof late this afternoon."

"Pushed?"

"Yeah. I came here straight from the hospital to search for incriminating evidence."

"You're sure he was pushed?"

"Positive."

"Who do you think pushed him?"

"The guy who owns Corral Construction. Brandon Corral. Heard of him?"

Brandon automatically straightened. Where had she gotten the harebrained notion that he was responsible for John's accident? Her crystal ball must be filled with liquid from the muddy waters of the Rio Grande!

Deciding to play along and pump her for information, he said, "I've heard Corral is—"

"An overbearing, arrogant, rich man's kid?"

"Something like that," Brandon agreed. He'd been called worse, but never by a woman. The women who'd chased after him substituted *masterful* for "overbearing," *confident* for "arrogant," and none of them objected to the idea of grabbing hold of his money with their little gold-digging hands. "Any man who'd hurt John has to be an SOB. Why do you think Corral did it?"

Molly grimaced. Unable to discuss business with her mother, she felt a compelling need to share her problem with someone who'd understand. Aside from being tall and handsome, he had a way of intently looking at her as though every word she said was extremely important to him.

"Corral bought out two of the three contractors who do the majority of work on the north side of Austin. He offered a bid on Winsome Plumbing, but John laughed at him. Obviously any competitor Corral can't buy he hospitalizes."

If Molly had been John's son, Brandon would have decked him. The urge to throttle her, or better yet grab her and kiss her until she was silent, had him shoving his thumbs beneath his belt buckle. Still, he felt obligated to defend his reputation. "That's a strong accusation, ma'am. Got any proof?"

"Plenty. Even though John was heavily sedated, he told me not to sell Winsome and to *get* Corral."

Brandon felt the blood drain from his face. He had made some wild threats to keep John alive. Maybe he'd been wrong to believe John's wavering smile meant John comprehended his ploy. Maybe the fragile bond of friendship was purely a figment of his imagination. Maybe John did hate him.

"I wouldn't worry about Corral if I were you," Brandon said, moving toward their parked trucks. "I'll make certain he doesn't bother you again."

Glad to have this man on her side, championing her cause, she asked, "You'll help?"

"Yes." Brandon opened the door of her truck and waited until she was in the truck before he closed her safely inside and replied, "I'm Brandon Corral. And I did not push John Winsome off that roof."

Molly clamped her teeth together to keep her jaw from dropping. He'd deliberately tricked her! She couldn't believe she'd been so damned gullible!

Concealed in the dark shadows of the truck, she gripped the steering wheel, fighting to control the impulse to resoundingly slap Brandon Corral's face. She would have to postpone the luxury of enjoying that wayward fantasy until later. He expected her to verbally lash out at him. To regain the business advantage she'd lost, she had to do the unexpected. She had to reverse the tables on him.

"I knew who you were when I saw you on the roof," she bluffed boldly. Smiling, she added, "I should have left you stranded up there, but out of my own innate goodness, I helped you down."

"You thought I worked for you."

"Corral, I know all my employees." She chuckled, a thin, reedy sound without humor. "Do you?"

"No," Brandon admitted, temporarily defeated. He detested being on the losing end of any business discussion. Never bested for long, he looked down at her feet and drawled softly, "I guess big isn't always best, huh?"

Molly cringed as though he'd slobbered on his finger and poked it in her ear. That low-down polecat had overheard her comment about her shoe size!

"I'm not the only one here who's several inches over the national norm, Corral." The sweet, melodic tones of her voice would have gagged a sugar-starved teenager. "You're the one who has to stoop to pushing an old man off a roof to conquer him."

"I did not push John," Brandon denied vehemently. "Can't you get that through your stubborn head?"

Feeling her confidence soar now that she'd convinced him she had known who he was from the beginning, she purred, "Next you'll be telling me you like my father."

"As a matter of fact, I climbed up on that roof in the middle of hurricane-force winds for that very reason. I do like John."

Molly laughed humorlessly. "Right, Corral. Why don't you mosey on back to your end of town and plan a ticker-tape parade for John when he gets out of the hospital?"

"I just might do that." He dared to lean forward, within striking distance. "By then John will have something to celebrate...the sale of Winsome Plumbing."

"By God, he'll never sell Winsome to you," she swore with vengeance in her voice.

Brandon smiled. Finally, the pendulum had swung and she was on the defensive. "Wanna bet those fancy emu-skin boots you're wearing?"

"Against that brand-new carpenter's belt buckled around your low-riding designer trousers?"

He extended his hand inside the cab of the truck. "You've got a bet. Your boots against my belt. Want the britches, too?"

Molly would have preferred to sink her teeth into his hand rather than shake it. Certain her palm was damp from clutching the steering wheel, she swiped it down the double-stitched seam of her jeans before she sealed the bet by placing her hand in his.

She expected a quick, knuckle-grinding handshake. Corral completely robbed her of breath by gently rotating his wrist, sliding her fingers until they draped over his fingers and then bringing her fingertips to his lips. The warmth from the tiny kiss he planted there traveled up her arm, expanding and magnifying in intensity. By the time it reached her heart it had the impact of the tiny blue flame of a blowtorch.

Her first impulse was to jerk her fingers away from the flame. She curbed it. Her second impulse was to trace the bow of his upper lip with the fleshy pad of her thumb. She curbed that, too. Corral took the decision-making option out of her hands by releasing her fingers.

"Cold hands, warm heart?" he drawled, his voice husky.

Molly had to blink twice to break the magical spell his touch had woven around her. Her mouth felt dry; her tongue, fuzzy. Her heart thumped against her ribs louder than an empty thirty-gallon metal drum being slammed on the rim with a ball-peen hammer.

But for her own peace of mind, she needed to get in the last word. "If it's warmth you're looking for—" she crooned as she picked up his woolly red blanket from the seat and tossed it through the window "—you'd be safer cuddling up inside this."

Molly tromped the gas pedal. As she turned the corner, she checked the rearview mirror. Brandon

Corral stood exactly where she'd left him, hands on his hips, legs spread apart, with his blanket *over his head*.

Chapter Three

At dawn, the Texas sun barely cast its illuminating rays inside Winsome's warehouse as Molly raised the door. During the fifteen-minute drive to work she'd tried to blame her sleepless night on worrying about her father, which was only partially true. Her Technicolor dreams had been of a tall, dark stranger, with eyes the hue of bittersweet chocolate and a wide carpenter's belt riding low on his hips. She'd awaken with the spare pillow clutched to her chest and an achiness at the juncture of her thighs.

Just goes to show what a poor judge of character I am, she castigated herself.

Each time she awakened, she reminded herself that Corral was the *enemy!* He was the man who'd pushed John, wasn't he? The same man who wanted to take

Winsome Plumbing away from her. He was the last man on earth she should allow to invade her dreams.

She refused to let thoughts of him continue to ruin her day. Briskly she strode to a shelving unit where several clipboards hung. The forms she'd designed to organize which crew went where each day were far less illuminating than the sun.

"They're blank," Molly groaned, flipping through the pages. "Blank!"

She slammed the clipboard on John's desk. She'd counted on these schedules for the information she needed to route the crews. Although she had a vague idea of what jobs the various subcontractor crews should be sent to from the paperwork she'd processed in the office, that "vague idea" wouldn't get the houses completed on schedule.

"Dammit, John."

Immediately she felt ashamed of herself for blaming her father. He had his way of doing things and she had hers. She made lists and flowcharts; John did, too. Only hers were stored on the computer's hard drive and his were stored in his computer-like mind.

She scowled at John's blank charts. Their lack of notations was the equivalent of a computer's hard-drive crash!

So much for her plan to arrive early and have the work schedules laid out for the crews. She'd have to rely on the men to tell her where they were supposed to be.

Talk about a backward way to run a construction business, she groaned inwardly. It was like putting a roof on a house with no slab poured.

The leather soles of her boots scuffed the concrete floor as she crossed into the corridor that led to her office. There had to be some way she could use the computerized data to narrow down the work in progress.

As she flicked on the light in her office, the solution came to her—check the supply lists in the data base. For lien-waver purposes, the supplier required the address of where the supplies would be used. And she had the addresses. That was a beginning. From the type of pipe, fittings and fixtures, she should be able to tell which phase of construction each project was in. She stepped on the surge-protector switch that activated her computer.

As the blue screen flickered, she thought of another avenue to follow. Each week the subcontractors—ground, top-out and finishing plumbers—turned in a draw to be paid. From the payroll entries she should be able to figure out where and what they'd completed.

Piecing the paper trail into sequential order and filling out John's blank charts from scratch would be time-consuming, but she had no choice. She hoped the men would be patient and allow her to fumble-butt around until John got back on his feet. They expected leadership. She had to provide it or...

The only "or" she could think of was Brandon Corral.

Molly made several rapid keystrokes on the keyboard. After she located the files she needed, she touched the print command. She wouldn't think about the consequences of not being able to fill her father's boots. And she sure as blazes wasn't going to waste time thinking about Corral's offer.

While the laser printer spouted out the first page, Molly glanced at the flagged map. Her father's yellow-and-gray flags had drawn the line of demarcation. By damned, she could hold it until he recuperated.

As she reached for the printout, the phone rang.

"Winsome Plumbing," she answered.

"How's your crystal ball doing this morning?" a familiar husky male voice inquired.

Think of the devil and conjure him up, Molly groaned silently, recognizing her adversary's sexy voice. Her finger hovered over the hold button on the telephone, but she refrained from punching it.

"My crystal ball is forecasting doom and gloom for Corral Construction," she snapped. "Anything I can do to help disaster strike?"

"That's why I called you."

"I don't need any disasters, thanks." She'd already had her daily dose.

"You have the damnedest way of twisting my words, Molly. I thought I was doing my good deed for the day by calling you and offering my help."

Molly laughed at the absurdity of the man who wanted to buy out her company, lock, stock and pipe wrench, offering to come to her rescue.

"Sure, Corral. You want to help—the way you helped John off that roof—headfirst."

"I didn't push John off the roof," Brandon argued through clenched teeth. He started to ask her what kind of man she thought he was and quickly changed his mind. There was little doubt that she'd be more than happy to recite his character flaws. "How is John?"

"Temporarily out of commission. Why? Are you having qualms?"

"No. Concern."

"What's wrong? Afraid Winsome Plumbing won't be worth buying out with me being the boss?"

"Sweetheart, I'm not obligated to buy your company. I can wait until Winsome Plumbing fails a few inspections or misses a few deadlines . . ."

"Speaking of *dead lines* . . ." Molly suddenly dropped the receiver into its cradle and grinned. "How's that one for dead?" she said to herself.

Brandon grimaced and banged down his receiver. Of all the sassy, ungrateful, stubborn women in Texas, Molly Winsome had to take the blue ribbon! No woman had ever spoken to him with such disrespect.

"Mrs. O'Connor! Get me the names of River Side's general contractors."

While he waited, Brandon tilted back his chair, his fingers steepled on his chest. He'd made it a practice to purchase only selected companies, ones undercapitalized or ones that had owners nearing retirement age. Winsome Plumbing fitted both specifications.

Nine years ago, after he'd finished his degree in construction management at the University of Houston, he'd devised a master plan based on Jake Corral's blueprint for success. Just as his grandfather had acquired small car agencies, consolidated them and built a financial empire, Brandon planned on following the same plan by merging the pop-and-son operations in the plumbing industry. Once they were consolidated, streamlined and operational, the purchasing power of Corral would drive down the costs of doing business and up the price paid per fixture that presently the general contractors arbitrarily dictated. Under his plan, the profit margin would soar and costs plummet.

Brandon resisted the urge to crack his knuckles as he thought of the one bugaboo between him and his goal—Winsome Plumbing. Losing the bid on the Bayou Oaks subdivision had been a major disappointment. He'd planned on squeezing Winsome's toes by demonstrating Corral's ability to underbid him.

Hell, he'd ruthlessly undercut his estimator's price ten percentage points and still lost. Negotiating a contract with each of the River Side's builders would be another exercise in futility as long as Molly Winsome continued to pump out below-cost bids.

Brandon leaned forward, elbows on his desk. Normally he played his cards close to his chest, but sometime in the near future he might give John a peek at his hand. Although he preferred a straight buyout, he might consider forming another company, a limited, *silent* partnership.

His secretary, a stout sixty-year-old with frizzy reddish gray hair and wire-framed glasses, entered his plush office, coffee cup in hand. She took one look at the vein throbbing on her boss's forehead and carefully placed the cup in front of him.

"I just read an article about stressed, single young men having heart attacks. When was the last time you took a vacation?"

Brandon drilled her with a scowl. He revised his last thoughts about Molly. She wasn't the only woman who lacked a filter between her brain and her mouth. Mrs. O'Connor had been bad-mouthing at him for years. He wasn't going to tolerate disrespect from Molly or his hired help.

"You're fired!"

"Again?"

"Permanently."

"Before or after I get those contractors' names?"

Fully aware that Mrs. O'Connor had a filing system that defied logic, Brandon pushed his swivel chair back from his desk. No point in cutting off his nose to spite his face, he decided. He'd never find those names.

"After."

"After you hire me back?" She smiled sweetly. "And give me a raise?"

"No raise."

Mrs. O'Connor shrugged her plump shoulders and turned toward the door to their connecting offices. "I told you the next time you got in a tizzy and fired me that you'd pay. No pay, no names."

"No games! Just get the damned file!" The door closing firmly behind her had the same definite click as a line going dead. "Mrs. O'Connor!"

He jumped to his feet and rounded his desk. Why didn't women fight fair? A man would belly up to him and threaten to punch his teeth down his throat. Women? They plastered smug smiles on their faces and hit a man where it hurt the most, in the wallet.

Brandon swung open the door, wanting to raise hell but knowing the devil wouldn't win if he took on Mrs.

O'Connor. He did the only smart thing a man could do under the present circumstances—he offered her a raise she couldn't refuse.

"I don't want your money. I want respect. No, I *demand* respect."

"You've got it, Mrs. O'Connor."

Sitting on the edge of her chair, spine as straight as a brick chimney, she nodded. "Here's the list you wanted and your telephone messages—a Mrs. Winsome phoned while you were on the other line."

"Don't worry, Mother. When Dad wakes up tell him I have everything under control," Molly said, feeling more confident as she glanced at the notations she'd made on John's previously blank charts. "Sorry to cut this short, but the men should be here any minute. I'll call again during lunch break."

"If you have time, be sure you return Mr. Corral's blanket."

Molly grinned. "I took care of that."

"You did?"

"Mother, I've got to run," she said as she heard a truck pull up to the warehouse. "The men are here to pick up supplies."

"I hope you told Mr. Corral how grateful we are for helping your dad."

"We'll talk about Mr. Corral later, Mother. Bye."

As she gathered up the papers strewn on her desk, she fervently hoped her father would correct Kate's erroneous impressions.

Corral only wanted one thing from John, and that wasn't friendship. He wanted John's plumbing company. And if yesterday's "accident" was an indicator, Corral would do *anything* to get it.

Determined to stop him at all costs, Molly scribbled a quick note to Yolanda, her secretary, regarding payroll. Not wasting another second of daylight, she hurried into the warehouse.

Burt, Cliff and Harold, one of the top-out crews that installed water pipe, stood toe-to-toe, deep in discussion. Their huddle broke in three opposite directions when they saw Molly striding toward them. Burt and Cliff started toward the rack of copper pipe; Harold moved toward the bed of his truck.

"Is what I heard true?" Burt asked. "Is the bossman laid up in the hospital?"

Molly nodded. "I'd like to run through these check sheets before you leave this morning."

"Where's the L-grade three-quarter-inch copper?" Cliff asked. "John said Western Supply would deliver it here late yesterday afternoon."

"Yeah. And the boxes of fittings," Harold added, ambling toward the bins where the copper fittings were supposed to be stored. "Are the tub valves being delivered today?"

Molly persisted, trying to get organized by saying, "Harold, you're finishing the house at 1228 Sunset, aren't you?"

"Finished that last week," he replied. "I started the 207 plan on Sand Creek."

Molly scanned her work schedule. Sand Creek was not listed. "What's the address?"

Scratching his untrimmed beard, Harold mumbled, "It's the second house on the right."

"You started that one?" Cliff asked, sounding surprised. "I thought John said you were supposed to do Pebble Lane, while my crew did that one."

Both men looked to Molly to solve the problem.

To her relief, she saw Cliff's name beside a Glenview address. "Cliff, you're scheduled for 805 Glenview."

Harold grinned; Cliff rolled his eyes. Burt emptied his fittings pouch into the bin.

"You sure you got the right address?" Cliff asked dryly.

She rechecked her list and admitted, "No."

"John said the roofers haven't finished that house. Guess I could start it, but you won't be able to get an inspection. You reckon that would work, Burt?"

Burt, the youngest of the three, shook his head. "You guys had better do what I'm doing."

"Whazzat?" Cliff asked.

"Unload Winsome's stuff off my truck. I heard Corral is hirin' for work in north Austin."

Stepping inside the triangle of bodies the three men had formed, Molly said, "You'd quit? With John flat on his back in the hospital?"

"John's the ramrod," Burt replied defensively. "Without him, Winsome will fall apart pronto."

Harold nodded. "I remember when John had his heart attack. He hired a superintendent and everything was Disasterville. Inspectors red-tagged every job we did." He gave the younger man a hard, thoughtful look. "Maybe you're right, Burt."

"Damned straight," Cliff agreed.

"Wrong!" Molly declared, slamming her clipboard against the bin's wooden slats. "I was in Dallas when John had his heart attack. I'm here this time.''

They were unconvinced, she thought, noticing none of the three could look her in the eye. Plumbers were notorious for pulling up stakes when the work was slow. Company loyalty and balsa wood had a lot in common—the least bit of stress and they both split.

Dammit, she'd shoot them in the knees with their own nail guns before she'd let them shuffle over to Corral with their hats in their hands, begging for a job!

"Nothing against you, Ms. Molly," Burt consoled. "I'm real sorry about John's accident and all, but I've got three youngsters to feed."

"As you pointed out, Harold, Winsome Plumbing had to pull itself up by its bootstraps once," Molly affirmed. "But if we work together, we'll be too busy making money to worry about our bootstraps."

"Yeah, the bill collectors will own them, too," Burt countered. "Sorry, but I can't risk being laid off."

Molly's stomach clenched into a hard knot as she watched Burt amble toward his truck. Her rah-rah pep talk equated to empty promises. None of the subcontractors wanted to quit. Conversely, none of them wanted to worry about their paychecks, either.

She wondered what Brandon Corral would do in a similar situation. Last night, he hadn't made empty promises. He'd snapped and snarled until he'd bullied her into moving the ladder.

Tearing a page out of his management book, she glared at the two remaining plumbers and said, "We don't have time to stand around chitchatting. Are you men working for Winsome, or am I going to put an ad in the *Austin Statesman*? I've got houses that need pipe in them. Make up your minds."

Harold and Cliff exchanged glances, slightly bewildered by her abruptness.

"John sent me to Jackson Street yesterday," Cliff said sheepishly. "He mentioned that Acme Pipe would deliver directly to the job site if they didn't get to the warehouse. I'll beep you on your pager if they're a no-show."

"I'll be right behind you," Molly assured him. Scowling at Harold she asked, "What about Sand Creek?"

"Nobody's gonna top-out that house but me," he replied, grinning from ear to ear. "Hey, Burt! You better get your buns back in here or Ms. Molly is gonna replace 'em!"

"With one of Corral's whiz kids," Molly snapped, her voice loud and clear. She crossed to the wall where the clipboards hung. "Starting today, I want your daily-report sheets filled out. I can't schedule work when I don't know what you've completed."

"Paperwork!" Harold grumbled.

"Sorry, men," she replied, not sounding the least bit apologetic. She pointed her pencil in Harold's direction. "You've heard John call me a paper brain and this clipboard helps my memory stick. If it's down in black and white, I won't forget it."

Cliff laughed and gigged Harold in the ribs. "Guess she's a chip off the old block."

"They make paper from wood chips, don't they?" Harold commented. "Your old man writes everything down on scraps of wood and tosses them in the back of his truck."

Burt, who had ambled back inside the warehouse and was quietly restocking his tool belt, joined in the camaraderie by saying, "Remember the apprentice plumber John threatened to lambast? He took John's pieces of wood and used them to wedge copper pipe into the studs."

"Yeah, John was cussin' like a ditchdigger while he went around prying his notes out of those holes." Cliff chortled. "Guess if John nicknamed Molly 'Paper Brain,' we'll have to start calling John 'Wooden Brain'!"

"Uh-huh. And directly after you call him 'Wooden Brain,' we'll be calling you 'No-Brainer' when John gets through with you," Harold drawled as he made the gesture of a head being unscrewed like a light bulb.

Cliff guffawed and took the clipboard. "Let's get truckin' before Ms. Molly gets on the phone and we're all called to stand in line to collect unemployment!"

There was no rancor in his words. By including her in their slightly off-color joke, Harold had informally dubbed her one of the "good ol' boys." Molly grinned happily as she glanced at her watch.

Seven o'clock, and all was well. Maybe not exactly "well," she amended silently, thinking of John. But definitely better.

By noon, she felt as though she'd been pulled through a knothole backward.

She'd wrangled with a plumbing inspector, the tile man and the roofer. And John's beeper, which she'd attached to the waist of her slacks, had beeped incessantly. When she read the message "Memory Full," she wished the damned thing would self-destruct.

"They'll have to wait," she murmured as she entered the hospital elevator.

After the door closed, she pressed the sixth-floor button.

Her stomach seemed to drop to her toes as the elevator zoomed upward nonstop. The flip-flop sensation reminded her of how she'd felt when she'd believed Corral was John's employee. She'd shined the flashlight in his face and her heart had fluttered as her pulse raced.

So he's handsome, she admitted silently.

He's a low-down snake, she corrected. A snake may be a handsome devil, but if you pick it up, don't yelp when he sinks his fangs into you! Those had been John's words of wisdom when she was a child.

Molly groaned. This entire morning she'd been preoccupied with Brandon Corral and his claim to be innocent of wrongdoing. The haunting possibility that she'd misjudged the man infuriated her. For some unknown reason, she had never been able to separate the poisonous "snakes" from the harmless "snakes."

By the laws of nature, her ex-husband should have slithered into her life. Instead Leon had sauntered into the office as though he owned the place. She'd taken one look at his immaculate white shirt, double-breasted suit and silk tie and mistakenly perceived him as a woman's answer to her maiden prayers.

Stuck in her analogy, she chafed her blue chambray shirtsleeve against her arm. Leon had wanted her to shed her old skin and let him mold her into his ideal woman. It had taken her five years to realize that without her own skin, she was just a hank of hair and a bag of bones.

She'd lost her identity. She was a nobody from nowhere, going nowhere. Worthless. Useless.

Her stomach settled as the elevator door swooshed open. As she stepped from the enclosure, Molly acknowledged the nurse on duty at the nurses' station with a nod, while mentally giving herself a shake by the scruff of her neck.

Molly Sloan no longer exists, she chided herself, only Molly Winsome. Pride raised her chin a fraction of an inch. She no longer had the trappings of wealth, but she had her self-respect.

Her chin dropped to her chest when she strode into John's room. There, big as you please, boldly signing John's cast with a black marker, was the man who had deliberately pushed John from the roof—Brandon Corral.

Chapter Four

"Are you certain you won't reconsider my first offer?" Brandon asked as he capped the pen John had given him and admired the Corral brand he'd drawn on Winsome's cast.

"Molly," her mother said, greeting her, then crossing the narrow room and bestowing a quick hug on her daughter.

Returning her embrace, Molly warily kept her eyes on her adversary. His grin jolted her heart, making it skip a beat. He stood with a pen in one hand, his other hand parting his sports coat where it rested on his denim-clad hip, and his brown eyes roamed over her in a lingering way that missed no detail.

He started at the tendrils of flame-colored hair the wind had blown loose, moved down the ivory-colored buttons of her **cha**mbray shirt, to the zipper of her snug-fitting jeans, down her long length of leg, to her fancy boots.

Instinctively Molly pressed her knees together as his gaze reversed, climbing upward, pausing on her slender waist, seeming to cup the fullness of her breasts beneath the concealing fabric. Her nipples hardened in response. .

Corral looked at her as though his fingers were an extension of his eyes.

She'd worked on construction sites since she was a teenager and not one man had dared to ogle her, especially in the presence of her father. Molly clenched her fists at her sides at the gleam of amusement in his sinful brown eyes as they met hers. He had good reason to laugh. While she'd been busting her buns taking care of business, Corral hadn't lost any time sneaking over to the hospital to make offers. The man had no shame!

"Hurrmph." John faked clearing his throat to get his daughter's attention. "How about a hug for your old, busted-up father?"

"Never old, Dad." Molly broke eye contact with Corral. She decided to treat him as though he were invisible. "Only injured. How are you feeling?"

"He slept through the night," Kate informed Molly before she teased her husband. "Snored so loudly they had to evacuate the men in the adjoining room."

As Molly lightly kissed his cheek, John chuckled. "A man thrown from a longhorn off the top of the state capitol has a right to snore."

Kate frowned. "Makes my blood boil to think how he'd be if Mr. Corral hadn't shown up and called an ambulance."

Startled by her mother's verification of Corral's claim of innocence, Molly glanced at John for confirmation.

John winced as he tried to sit up.

"Push the button, John," Kate said, rushing to her husband's side and raising the bed for him. After she'd fluffed his pillow she turned toward her daughter. "Mr. Corral said you two met last night in Wood Hollow."

John chuckled again and nodded. "Said he'd still be hanging on to that chimney if it wasn't for Molly. Guess she partially repaid the debt I owe you, huh, Corral?"

"Consider your debt paid in full," Brandon agreed, returning the pen to John.

Molly heard how Corral had stressed "your debt" and inwardly cringed. Did he think she owed him an apology for her accusation? The look of anticipation, written clearly on his handsome face, confirmed her suspicion.

Unwilling to accept the remotest possibility that she'd been defensive, Molly said, "He led me to believe he was one of our men."

"That was after she accused me of pushing you from the roof," Brandon explained, affecting a pained expression. He took a seat near the side of the bed.

Reluctant to continue the compromising discussion further in front of her parents, she glared at Corral and asked, "Would you mind stepping out into the corridor, Mr. Corral?"

Brandon glanced at his watch, then extended his hand toward John. "It's been a pleasure, sir. I'm glad you're on the road to recovery."

"Two weeks. Doc Aspenwald says I'll be up and around on crutches by then." John pumped his hand, then winced and lightly rubbed the sheet over his bandaged ribs. "Thanks for offering to help Molly over the rough spots. I'll rest easier knowing she can depend on you."

"What?" Molly squawked in protest. "Me? Depend on him? Dad—talk about putting a fox in the henhouse!"

John held his ribs and chuckled anew; Kate scowled.

"Have you forgotten that he's the man who wants to take over Winsome Plumbing—" Molly warned.

"Excuse me," a nurse interrupted from the doorway. "Are you ready for lunch, Mr. Winsome?"

"Shall we?" Brandon asked, unmoved by her allegation. He circled the end of the hospital bed. "No point in upsetting John while he's having lunch."

Molly felt the warmth of his hand at her elbow as Corral steered her toward the door. Deciding to take up the matter with her parents when they were not under Corral's influence, she muttered, "Let go of my arm." More loudly she said, "I'll talk to you all later. Love you, Dad, Mom."

She'd marched halfway down the corridor before she cleared her throat, as though she'd swallowed a cup of sawdust, and said, "I suppose you think I owe you an apology."

"For your telephone manners, your character assassination or your accusations?" When they reached the elevator, he touched the down button. "Well? Which one?"

"An apology made under duress is like a contract signed with a six-shooter held to the head." The doors parted. Molly broke his hold. Head held high, she preceded him into the cubicle. "Invalid."

"You don't just give up gracefully, do you?" he snapped.

Molly drew herself up to her full seventy inches in height and still had to tilt her head upward to look him in the eye. "Nobody intimidates me."

"That I can believe," Corral said sarcastically.

Simultaneously, they both reached for the elevator button, but his reflexes were quicker. Her index finger mashed his.

"Sorry," she automatically responded, jerking her finger away as though it had been burned. "Look, Corral, maybe I jumped to a few conclusions."

"A few?"

"Several," she conceded, the fight draining out of her. She focused on the descending numbers. She couldn't look at him without remembering those damned dreams. In reality, would his lips gently kiss her? Or would they press hard, punishing kisses for the accusations she'd made? "You have to admit, they were logical assumptions."

He lifted one dark eyebrow. Amusement lit his eyes. "I do?"

She could feel him glaring at her. And she could feel her involuntary responses. Her cheeks tingled, but not with shame; with an awareness of the sinking sensation in her stomach that was not due to the rapid descent of the elevator.

"Last night the doctors had heavily sedated Dad before I talked to him. He spoke your name. Said—" she wiggled two fingers to indicate quotation marks "—'get him...hell.' What message would you get if you pieced that information together?"

"Get Corral and send him straight to hell," Brandon admitted. Considering the wild threats he'd made to keep John's blood pumping, he wondered if Molly's interpretation was incorrect. Maybe he was the one who should be apologizing.

Molly paused at the conciliatory note in his voice. Through a blaze of red eyelashes, she surreptitiously looked at Corral. His chocolate-colored irises had rims of navy blue, which gave his eyes a piercing look. Or perhaps it was the bronze of his skin tone that set off his eyes and made him appear exceedingly dangerous.

She caught him giving her the same kind of scrutiny and said, "You can imagine how foolish I felt last night when I found out I had helped the man my father had condemned."

"Would you have moved the ladder if I'd told you who I was?"

"Probably..."

"Not," Brandon injected into her pause.

Molly shrugged. "You should have told the truth."

"Straightforwardness?" Brandon scoffed. "I seem to recall trying that earlier in the day. One more chorus of 'Friends in Low Places' and I would have headed for the Oasis to find out what I've been missing."

"That's apples and oranges. You can't compare my leaving you dangling on the phone with..."

"Leaving me dangling on a roof?"

Irritated by the way he finished her sentences by twisting her words to his advantage, she asked, "Is it true men demonstrate their desire for superiority by never letting a woman finish what she started to say?"

"Is it true women change the subject when they're losing an argument?" Brandon countered.

"That wasn't why I asked you about male superiority." The doors opened, but Molly stood her ground. To justify her claim, she added, "You can't compare being put on hold with not identifying yourself. One was a delaying tactic and the other a deliberate lie."

"Going up?" an intern dressed in green surgical garb asked with a cordial smile.

"Out," Brandon replied, crossing Molly's back with his arm and firmly grasping her by the upper arm as he ushered her into the lobby. "You never asked my name. I could have let you drive off without being any the wiser."

"Why didn't you?"

Her defiant eyes locked on the pulse beat at the base of his throat. With each heartbeat, she felt a pulse where his fingers circled her arm. Because of his height, she had to keep her arm away from her side, or his knuckles would skim the side of her breast. Her defiance lost its edge as his thumb cocked, grazing the thin fabric of her shirt; the fleshy pad soothed the spot he'd tightly held.

Brandon thoughtfully tried to compose a safe reply. Why hadn't he been content to let her leave without knowing his identity? Simple. He'd felt guilty about being unable to help John and guilty about the things he'd said to him. And he'd felt like a prize idiot for getting stranded. But none of those reasons justified his behavior.

The responses she evoked from him were intangible, nothing specific that he could identify. From their first telephone conversation she had intrigued him. Maybe it was the comment he'd overheard her make about her shoe size. Or maybe it was watching the long length of her legs as she competently dodged the piles of rubbish. Or maybe it was how she wouldn't back down from a fight, even when the odds were against her.

Vulnerability, gracefulness and pure sass, he thought, summing up his impressions of Molly. For totally illogical reasons, that rare combination appealed to him.

It's what made him reject the safety net of anonymity.

He'd wanted her to know his name.

The flip side being that he wanted to know her, he concluded. Self-preservation instincts warned Brandon to hide his irrational feelings behind a mask of male arrogance. To do otherwise would be to expose a weakness she'd use against him.

Brandon dropped his arm and widened the distance between them before he grinned a cocky, self-confident smile and teased, "I didn't want you searching through Winsome's employee records, trying to track me down."

"Of all the conceited . . . presumptuous . . . egotistical. . ." Molly sputtered, folding her arms across her chest to rub the warmth of his touch off her skin.

"The only reason I'd be inclined to track you down is to collect that carpenter's belt you owe me."

His smile faded. "Our bet is on temporary hold, since I gave my word to John that I'd help you until he has recovered."

Silently Molly added "reneger" to her growing list of Corral's personality flaws. Intent on keeping pace with him, she barely noticed her truck until she'd passed by the lopsided rear bumper. Molly shoved her hand inside her jeans pocket to get her keys. With his monumental ego she felt confident he'd believe her when she said, "I'll call you if I need help..."

As he watched those long legs of hers disappear into the cab of the truck, Brandon finished her sentence. "Don't call me?"

Not unless your taste in music has changed, she replied silently.

She shut the door, started the engine and shifted into reverse, all the while praying John's temperamental truck would cooperate.

A snort, buck and a backfire later, she inched backward. She popped the clutch and shifted into first gear. The truck wheezed, then inched forward to where Corral stood.

"Sounds as though your truck is on its last legs." Afraid she'd get stranded at some isolated job site, Brandon said, "There's a truck at my warehouse you can borrow."

"With Corral Plumbing branded on the side of it?" Molly lifted one eyebrow when he nodded. Rumors would fly faster than shingles in a tornado if she rode up to a Winsome plumbing site behind the wheel of a Corral truck. "No, thanks. I'll change Betsy's plugs when I get around to it."

Jogging to keep up with the slow pace of the truck, Brandon huffed, "Is there anything mechanical that you can't do?"

"Just call me Wonder Woman," she snapped, mentally scoring a point against his Superman wise-crack.

She gunned the engine and careered off the parking lot when she remembered bopping a neighborhood boy for calling her that same name. Wonder Woman was an Amazon, six feet tall and strong as a hod carrier. She detested any reference to her size.

Molly bit the soft inner lining of her lip and wished she'd kept her mouth shut.

Corral had no way of knowing her defense mechanisms of laughter and a sharp tongue were the direct result of the shame and humiliation of being the tallest girl with the biggest feet, from kindergarten through high school. He had no way of knowing that none of the boys in grade school thought the copper pipe guns she manufactured in John's garage were the coolest weaponry in their arsenals. Those same boys became young men who never remembered her when it came to dates and dances, but they all brought their jalopies to her to be fixed—free. She'd been ripe for the picking when her ex-husband had tried to change her from a tomboy into a socialite.

Yeah, she bragged about her mechanical ability. She was damned proud of it. But she'd drop sideways through a manhole before she mentioned it again to Corral.

* * *

Two hectic days later, Molly felt completely frazzled as she confronted the counter clerk at the supply house. Her hand trembled with exhaustion as she held the invoice. "What is this, Matt? Nail plates—two cents apiece higher than last month?" Before he could reply, she pointed to the number beside the boxes of fittings delivered. Her voice was as cold as the freon running through metal pipe to an air conditioner as she asked, "Since when do you cut my order?"

"We're expecting a shipment next week." Matt's beefy hand stroked his scruffy blond beard nervously as he glanced up at the man who'd come through the door and stood directly behind her. "I could call the store in San Antone to see if they have any nineties in stock."

"Do that. I'll drive there if I have to. I can't put copper pipe together with glue."

"Your truck won't make it that far," Brandon said, moving beside her and leaning against the high counter. Dark smudges beneath her vibrant blue eyes and the pronounced hollows under her cheekbones unsettled him. "Check my order. Take what she needs from it."

Matt nodded. "Yes, sir. Molly, if you'll excuse me, I'll have to go to the loading dock to have them unloaded from the delivery truck."

"What about those price increases?" she haggled, unconcerned about arguing over pennies in front of Corral.

"I'll adjust your bill," Matt agreed affably.

Molly folded the invoice and stuck it in her shirt pocket while she mustered a smile of gratitude. "Thanks."

"You're welcome. You can return the favor by sparing me one hour from your busy schedule." His face softened into a smile. "It would have taken you three times that long to drive to San Antone and back."

Unconsciously she rubbed her neck, trying to loosen the knotted muscles caused by too much stress, too much work and too little peace of mind. She needed a break. From dawn to long beyond dark she'd lived and breathed Winsome Plumbing.

"Where to?" she asked when he captured her hand and tucked it in the crook of his arm.

He'd propelled her through the door and into his truck before he asked, "Have you eaten today?"

"I grabbed a sandwich out of one of the machines at the hospital."

"A gastronomical delight," he commented.

A smile tugged Molly's lips and the lines of strain bracketing her mouth disappeared. "The taste did resemble sawdust, but it was filling. I'm not hungry. Really."

Brandon took her at her word as he drove toward Barton Springs. Midweek, the park wouldn't be crowded. Once she'd relaxed and no longer ran on raw energy, her appetite might be restored.

During the short ride Molly began to unwind. Without asking, she knew he must be taking her to one of the parks. Although she could think of a dozen places she needed to be, she kept silent. She turned off the pager clipped to her belt. Later, she'd feel guilty about wasting precious minutes from her workday.

Brandon parked under the boughs of a century-old oak tree. A short distance away thickets of willow and an occasional granite boulder studded the banks of the clear springwater. He could have brought up the fight Austinites had waged to save the springs from developers, but he decided that topic would lead to her thinking about business. Instead he took her hand and followed the path toward the water.

With a sigh of pleasure, Molly sat down on a flat boulder and dispensed with her boots and socks. She pulled up the legs of her jeans to avoid getting them wet. As she dangled her toes in the chilly stream, she leaned back on her cocked elbows and let the sun wash her face with sunlight.

Brandon watched with something close to fascination. The smile of appreciation she cast him made his heartbeat quicken. Molly's lack of artificial inhibition appealed to him. He wished it had been his touch that had brought the sensual softening to her mouth.

She dipped her feet deeper with a paddling motion, letting the water climb to midcalf and invigorate her while she watched Brandon. He seemed hypnotized by the water swirling around and over the rocks, gurgling as it splashed into the bluish green deep water.

For one crazy moment, he considered sitting behind her, letting her lean her head against his chest. She could use his thighs as an armrest while he brushed aside the heavy coil of braided hair and kissed the line of tense muscles along her neck.

"Brandon?"

"Yeah?" To dispel his daydream, he dropped on one knee, scooped up a handful of water and doused his face. "Brrrrrr!"

"I thought you were going to jump in."

He hunkered down close to Molly, but he didn't crowd her. As he cast off his shoes and socks, she was mildly surprised by her growing curiosity about him. Aside from rescuing her father and amassing a fortune in the trades, who was Brandon Corral? What made him tick? She stared at him, as though he had question marks indelibly stamped on his forehead.

Her inquisitiveness was palpable to Brandon. Since he doubted she'd given him a second thought before now, her interest pleased him.

"Go ahead. Ask," he encouraged as he reclined next to her. "What do you want to know?"

Molly smiled, rolled to her side so she could see his face and answered simply, "Everything."

"In less than an hour?" he retorted, chuckling. He tugged the end of the thick braid, which had fallen across her shoulder.

"Hit the peaks, skip the valleys."

"Okay." Before she could protest, his fingers nimbly removed the rubber band that held the braid in place. "I'm thirty-two. A graduate of UT's business school. Single—"

"Why?" She interrupted him at the point she found most interesting.

"No specific reason."

She wasn't going to let him get off that easily. "I imagine you've sown your share of wild oats."

"Cautiously," Brandon promptly qualified. "There are too many unwanted children for me to add to the problem."

The hollowness of his tone of voice alerted her to a hidden meaning. "Oh? Did you feel unwanted as a child?"

He'd revealed more than he'd intended, but it didn't matter. "Sometimes. My parents travel constantly."

"So who raised you?"

"I lived with my grandfather."

She noticed he'd closed his eyes, as though closing the subject.

"I've had my share of infatuations. But sex and love aren't one and the same, are they?"

Molly wrinkled her nose. "No. I learned that lesson the hard way."

"You're married?" He dropped the silky skein of hair he'd unwoven as though the strands burned his fingers.

"Divorced." She saw the relief spread across his face before she explained, "Nobody's fault. No good guys. No bad guys. We just didn't have much in common."

He sensed she'd understated how she truly felt. "No regrets?"

"Perhaps," she admitted. The corners of her lips drooped. "Failure is always laden with remorse, isn't it?"

"I wouldn't know," he replied, purposely sounding cocky to make her laugh. He lifted her hair, letting it cascade to her shoulder, engrossed by the way the sunshine lit it with flames of red. "I never consider the possibility of failure. Ups and downs. Minor glitches. Setbacks. Yeah, I've experienced all of those, but never the F word."

Grinning, she sat up. It was warm on the slab of rock where they sat. Almost hot. The breeze had died. She hiked her jeans above her knees and eased into the knee-deep water.

"I wish we'd brought our swimsuits," she said, gasping as her hot skin slid into the icy water. "Once you get used to it, the water feels great."

If they hadn't been at a public park, she would have suggested stripping down to their underwear. There was barely any difference between her lingerie and a bikini.

The glint of devilment she saw in Brandon's dark eyes warned her that he'd had a similar thought. When he stood up, unbuttoned his shirt, yanked it from his waistband and dropped it, she shook her head.

The movement of her head, combined with the current pushing against her knees and swirling around her legs, made her dizzy. Slick rocks under her feet shifted beneath her tender feet. Her arms flailed as she lost her balance.

"Whoooa!"

Instantly she felt Brandon's arms around her, holding her upright until she recovered her balance. Laughing, she clung to his shoulders while he scooped her into his arms.

"You're soaked," he said, teasing her by lowering his arms until her backside was only inches from the water.

Molly wound her arms tightly around his neck. "You wouldn't!"

"Wouldn't I?"

With her face burrowed against his, her breasts flattened against his bare chest, her hair blanketing his arm in silk, a shaft of desire speared him, weakening his knees.

"No! You wouldn't," Molly said, catching the lobe of his ear between her teeth, giving it a sharp little nip.

She felt a light tug on her scalp. Her neck arched to relieve the slight pressure. Their eyes met. His were hot, smoldering, intent, as they dropped to focus on her parted lips.

He wanted to kiss her. Of that she had no doubt. And she would not have objected. She was sure of that, too.

He smiled suddenly, a crooked slant of his lips, and his thumb and forefinger massaged her neck. Proud of himself for being able to control his lust, he waded to the bank.

"My hour is up. I'd better get you back to your truck before it turns into a pumpkin." He chuckled. "Come to think of it, a pumpkin is probably more roadworthy."

Molly's pager beeped. She removed the communication gadget from her belt, pushed the small white button and read the phone number. Immediately she turned into a gas station when she recognized the office number with 911 behind it. From the ashtray she took a quarter and rushed to the telephone.

"Hell's a poppin'," Yolanda said when she recognized Molly's voice. "You'd better get over to Wood

Hollow. The building inspector flunked the top out and the super is hopping mad. He'd scheduled it for the drywall crew tomorrow.''

"Did he say why it flunked?"

"Wrong grade of copper. The super wants the M-grade ripped out and replaced with L-grade copper by morning."

"Check your payroll records and see who did the work. I'll have to pull them off the job they're on to correct the mistake."

"I did. It's that new crew John fired last week. Mickey Kasper.''

Molly groaned a foul, potty-mouth curse, one appropriate for her trade. "I should have walked that building before the inspector arrived."

"Don't be so hard on yourself, Molly. You inspecting the building wouldn't have magically changed the green lines on the copper pipe to red lines.''

"No, but I could have called off the afternoon inspection.'' John's flawless record with the building department receiving a black mark concerned Molly. Unless she got on top of what took place in each building, the inspectors would nitpick every piece of pipe and fixture Winsome Plumbing installed. Wouldn't Corral love to see Winsome Plumbing drown in a sea of red tags? He'd be on the phone with the other general contractors quicker than flies on road apples. "I'll take care of it."

"How?''

Molly did a mental inventory of the boxes of fittings in John's truck. "Call the supplier and order three hundred feet of L-grade half- and three-quarter-inch pipe. I want it delivered to the job immediately."

"Burt's crew is over at Barton Creek. Do you want me to beep him?"

"No." Burt would empty his van and drag up if she pulled his men off their work. She also rejected the idea of having Yolanda call in a backup crew. Time prohibitive, she concluded silently.

"It's been a few years since I traded in my torch for a computer program, but I'm still a licensed plumber. I can do it."

"By yourself?" Yolanda squeaked in disbelief. "By morning?"

"I'll string lights if I have to. Call in the house for a reinspection first thing tomorrow morning." She glanced at her watch, then at the sun high overhead. She had six hours of daylight maximum. It would take an hour or so to remove the wrong copper pipe and at least five to string and repipe. She'd be cutting it close, but she could do it. "And, Yolanda, don't page me again unless the warehouse explodes. Just take messages and tell whoever phones that I'll phone back first thing tomorrow morning."

"I think we should call John."

"Don't."

"But..."

"Don't," Molly repeated emphatically. "John can't pipe a building from his hospital bed. Do what I said and call the supplier. Between the two of us, we'll take care of this problem. I'll see you in the morning."

Molly hung up the phone before Yolanda could lodge another protest and darted back to the truck.

As she made a U-turn and sped toward the highway, she excused Yolanda's lack of faith in her competence to get the pipe installed. Yolanda had been hired while Molly had been in Dallas. The woman's reservations undoubtedly stemmed from listening to John's favorite water-drenching stories about his daughter's early attempts at being a plumber's helper.

The summer she'd turned sixteen, bored and lonely, she'd nagged, begged and cajoled John until he'd allowed her to tag along with one of the crews. Then she'd nagged, begged and cajoled the plumbers until they'd let her solder water pipe. When the building was tested, the piping would have caused envy in the heart of every fireman in Austin. Water sprinkled profusely throughout the building; there were so many leaks in the pipe it could have doused a three-alarm fire in record time.

Molly smiled as she recalled John's tale of woe. She gave him full credit for turning a "fireman's dream" into a "damned fine plumber." She had her journeyman's license shortly after graduating from high school, and her master's license four years later. Official state records listed Molly Winsome as one of the youngest licensed plumbers on a printout where feminine names were as scarce as solid gold faucets in a tenement house.

"Can-do," Molly said, abbreviating "I can do it" to a single word. It had become her motto.

A backbreaking hour later, she hauled the last twenty-foot lengths of copper pipe to the back of her truck. What couldn't be cut up and used as stub-outs on another job, she'd sell to the scrap yard. As she sorted through the toolbox for the fittings she'd need, she kept a sharp eye on the road for the delivery truck.

"It should have been here by now," she grumbled, swiping a long wisp of hair back from her face.

"By golly, if it isn't Ms. Molly," a framing carpenter shouted from the building across the street.

"Hey, Milton," she called, grinning at the broad-shouldered, slim-hipped, long-haired carpenter swinging down from the rafters as though he'd been born in a tree. He was never one to hurry, she remembered, watching his loose-gaited swagger as he crossed the muddy yard and street. "How's it going?"

"Mighty fine. You sure are a sight for sore eyes, Coppertop. How many years has it been since you were pushing pipe up my scrawny butt to get me movin' faster? Three? Four?"

Automatically she tucked her foot on the running board of the truck and leaned against it to minimize the difference in their heights. Milton was muscular, but short. "Closer to six."

"Six years." He used his fingers like a wide-toothed comb to dislodge tiny flecks of sawdust from his blond hair. "Heard you were back at Winsome's runnin' the office. What are you doin' here? Did the electrical storm last night fry your computer?"

"John took a bad fall. I'm taking up the slack until he's out of the hospital."

"Damn, I'm sorry to hear that. He gonna be okay?"

"Sure. You know John. He's tough."

"It's been a while since the sweat off your brow earned you an honest dollar," he teased, picking up a short piece of scrap pipe and tossing it up in the air; it spiraled end over end, then he deftly caught it. "But don't you have this backward? Aren't you supposed to be putting pipe in the building, instead of carting it out?"

"I needed the practice," Molly joked feebly.

She followed the path of his gaze as it moved to the red sticker displayed prominently on the front window.

"Uh-oh."

She shrugged and explained, "New crew. Wrong grade of pipe. It happens."

"Anything I can do to help?"

Molly shook her head and expressed her gratitude by punching him lightly on his muscular biceps. "I appreciate the offer, but I'm stuck until the supplier makes a delivery."

"While I was up there putting that last header on I noticed a truck delivering pipe a couple of streets over there." He turned toward the opposite end of the subdivision and shielded his eyes from the strong midafternoon sun. "It's Corral's job, but I reckon nobody would mind you appropriatin' a couple of lengths. Just to get you started, until your delivery truck arrives."

If it had been Fontenout's job, she would have been over there quicker than a flintstone striker making sparks. Molly shifted from one foot to the other as she put herself in Corral's shoes. What would she do if he came begging for pipe?

"You'd give it to him," Milton said, reading her mind and watching her worry her bottom lip.

Yeah, I'd give it to him. Literally. He'd have a crease down the center of his head from where she "gave" it to him.

"I'll wait," she decided. "The truck ought to be here any minute."

"Whatever you say, Coppertop." Milton tossed the pipe he'd held in the truck bed and gave her a consoling pat on the shoulder. "Give me a shout if you need help unloading it."

"Can-do. Good talking to you."

She straightened, putting both feet on the pavement as she watched him walk away from her. Unbidden, her mind elongated Milton's swaggering backside to the size of a taller man. Last night, she had mistaken Corral's identity, but not his occupation. Only a man in the trades could perfect that strut.

Catching herself daydreaming about Brandon Corral, she slapped one hand against her thigh, annoyed by her lack of control. She glanced from the M-grade copper she'd removed to the street where a ready supply of the correct-grade copper had been delivered.

Three o'clock, she noted, checking out the time. Each sweep of the hand on her watch meant the chances of her getting her building finished and ready for inspection lessened. She rose on tiptoe, hoping to catch a glimpse of Acme's red delivery truck.

She considered going to a phone and calling the supplier, but discarded the notion. Should the truck arrive while she was gone, the driver wouldn't dump a load of costly pipe on the ground. He'd think he had the wrong address and return to the warehouse.

Then where would she be? She'd never finish before dark by the time the pipe was rerouted.

Her searching gaze returned to the skeletal frames of Corral's buildings. Chances were his men only planned on stringing the building today, preparing it for an early-morning start, she rationalized, since she knew most subcontractors started at seven and quit by three. Corral's men would be hanging it up for the day shortly.

They didn't really *need* the pipe. She did. After they left, she could use what they hadn't strung in the rafters. Before dawn, she could replace it with stock from Winsome's warehouse.

Molly gave herself a mental shaking to stop the same type of thinking every thief in Austin used. Her needing Corral's pipe did not justify taking it without permission.

She ground her teeth in an effort to halt the next logical idea—call Corral. He'd told John he would help her.

Heaving a deep sigh as the idea forced its way to the front of her consciousness, she kicked her tire and muttered, "What choice do I have?"

None. She could waste precious minutes waiting for the delivery truck or call Corral. "Or sweet-talk his men into loaning me some until tomorrow?" she mused aloud, liking this option. "Corral never need know."

Having found a temporary solution to her problem, she jumped into her truck and drove Betsy toward Corral's job site. Her conscience nagged at her, but she had a swift reply. Sneaky, yes, but no sneakier than his going behind her back to the hospital.

She'd bet that her arrival spoiled some under-handed, devious plan Corral had formulated to bilk her father out of his business.

Molly smacked the steering wheel, cursing her bad luck as she got within sight of the pile of pipe. There, parked beside it, was Corral's damned shinier-than-new Suburban. As much as her pride demanded that she stick her nose in the air and cruise past his truck, Molly's practicality demanded she stop.

Vanity, pride's handmaiden, compelled her to glance in the mirror before bounding from the truck. What she saw would have appalled her ex-husband. Women weren't supposed to leave their home with no trace of lipstick or makeup and with their hair sticking out like barbed wire painted red. She knew the litany by heart.

As she tugged the door handle and pushed against the door, she paraphrased the immortal words of a true Southern gentleman by declaring staunchly, "Frankly, I don't give a damn! I need that pipe.

"Corral!" she shouted, cupping her hands around her mouth to make her voice carry over the pounding of hammers. "Hey. Corral."

Brandon nodded at Bob Nelson, the crew's fore-man, and sidestepped through the upright studs until he reached the shadowed wraparound front porch of what would soon be a Texas Victorian two-story.

They were standing less than twenty feet apart; he could feel the heat of her temper before her voice rose as she called his name for the third time. He also felt a tightness in his thighs and buttocks. Even with her fists clenched and her face flushed with angry color, Molly Winsome was one gorgeous redhead.

She wore the same clothes he'd studied in the picture at his office, but once again he acknowledged that the photograph by no means depicted how beautiful she really was. In real life her softly rounded breasts, tiny waist and slender hips accentuated her long, long legs.

Smiling, he stepped from the shadows into the sunlight and sauntered toward her. "Do you want me?"

His innocent question provoked a not-so-innocent response inside Molly. Corral had a smile that made her insides quiver!

Strap 'em down, she thought, wishing a J-hook could quiet her jangling nerves.

"Pipe," she croaked, her throat parched. She licked her lips. Her tongue felt like emery cloth scratching a smooth metal surface. "I need some pipe."

"How much?" he asked, pleased that Molly had come to him to ask a favor. His smile broadened until it reached his eyes.

"All of it."

Brandon lazily stepped forward, invading her wide perimeter of private space and scaling the invisible wall Molly hid behind. His eyes held a subtle gleam when the distance between their chests shrank to inches. If either of them took a deep breath, her chest would touch the pockets of his shirt.

"It's yours for the taking."

Molly mentally substituted "I'm" for "it's" and made the unfortunate mistake of inhaling deeply. She smelled the spicy scented soap he'd used to shower, heard the rasp of cotton across cotton, and felt her knees weaken, as though her breasts had touched his bare chest. She defied the submissive feminine urge to drop her chin; she raised it until her eyes were level with his.

"On one condition," Brandon stipulated with a sexy drawl.

Chapter Five

"Let me help you," Brandon offered, before she turned on her heel and strode away from him. "In exchange for my services, have dinner with me."

The devil must have murmured that same incantation in Eve's ears before she accepted the shiny apple, Molly thought—Winsome being the equivalent of Paradise to her. Would she be banned from it if she took a teeny bite, a tiny bit of help from the man who wanted her company? His offer was tempting, very tempting, as were his lips, which smiled devilishly only a kiss away from her own.

A horn blaring as the delivery truck she waited for pulled to the curb saved Molly from yielding to temptation.

"Got your pipe, Ms. Molly," the driver called. "Do you want it dropped here or at the address Yolanda called in to the supply house?"

Fate, thy name is Acme Pipe Supply, Molly thought, her heart drumming wildly against her rib cage.

"Drop it at the address, Sal," she called over her shoulder. "I'll be right with you to help unload it."

Sal waved and gunned the gas pedal.

"Your men can unload it," Brandon yelled over the rattle of pipe clanging together. Disgruntled by the untimely intrusion on their conversation, he said, "You and I need to have a serious talk."

"I'm not selling Winsome. End of serious talk."

Molly pivoted on one foot to whirl away from him, and tripped trying to avoid his feet. He put his hands on her waist to steady her. It was a reflexive movement, the sort of thing any man would do to prevent a woman from falling. Brandon realized as he snugly secured Molly in the safety of his arms and saw the sultry dilation of her pupils that the sparks of sexual tension bombarding his senses had exploded with the force of a lit gas main.

Every muscle in his body felt stone hard as she felt him quicken against her. The humid air between them hummed with an electrical charge. She held his gaze, mesmerized, unable to move.

Brandon rocked his taut thighs against her, leaving no room for her to mistake his blatant body language. Her eyes widened as she received his silent message. With her inclination to jump to the wrong conclusions, he decided to be brutally frank.

"Right now, it's you I want, Molly. To hell with Winsome and Corral Plumbing."

She saw his intent; his dark eyes with their flared navy rims had moved to her lips. She jerked her head to one side, refusing to submit and at the same time exposing the vulnerable curve of her throat to him.

He blew away the threads of silky auburn hair caught in the collar of her shirt, then caught a tiny section of her pale flesh between his teeth, giving her a nip. A butterfly kiss healed the bite.

"You need my help," he whispered against the base of her neck. "Why won't you admit it?"

She scrubbed the moist heat of his mouth from her neck with the back of her hand. Only one other man had instinctively known how sensitive, how responsive, her neck was to the slightest caress. "I don't need you."

Molly felt certain she'd hit him where it hurt when his smoky-brown eyes changed to slate black. She'd come too close to capitulating, to letting him seal a personal victory with a kiss. Luckily she had the good sense to back off from the storm brewing in his eyes.

By damned, he wasn't going to allow her to have the last word this time. His long legs veritably ate up the ground between them. For a man who abhorred violence against women, his fingers came close to brutality when they caught her wrist and swung her around.

He anticipated her other hand taking a roundhouse swing at him; he blocked it, then he cuffed it with his thumb and forefinger.

In a voice no louder than a fierce breeze he whispered, "That's a lie and we both know it. What are you *really* afraid of, Molly Winsome?"

You. Me. Who you are and what I am, she confessed silently. She wondered if Corral was ever susceptible to doubts or fears or regrets. He seemed to be able to focus his strong-willed determination on one goal—acquisition. Attaining his goal justified any means—even sexual chemistry.

She had to rile him to hide her weakness. To do otherwise would invite a tormenting, stormy emotional entanglement. She wouldn't permit herself to be vulnerable to any man ever again. To keep her father's company intact, she had to harden her heart against Brandon Corral.

"Nothing. Certainly not you," she snapped. "I'd appreciate it if you'd stop manhandling me and get the hell out of my way. I have a building to pipe."

"Our talk will be personal, not business related." His thumb and forefinger parted. Only his eyes held her in place. "Your top-out crew has the pipe. They can start without you."

Her heart gave a funny lurch, like an old pump being primed. Clogged by years of built-up distrust, she chose to disregard his reference to a personal talk and heard only the conclusion he'd drawn. He believed she had a crew to do the work. She certainly wasn't going to discourage that notion. The last man on earth she wanted to have see the inspector's red sticker pasted in the front window was Brandon Corral!

Molly tried to forget the wounded look in Corral's eyes as she departed without responding to his personal invitation. It had only been revealed for mere seconds. If she'd blinked, or broken eye contact before she stepped backward toward her truck, she wouldn't have noticed it.

She'd seen the same flare of dark pupils in her own eyes when sitting in front of the vanity mirror, listening to her ex-husband belittle her.

Hurt?

Was that what she'd seen?

A second later, Brandon had flashed her a cocky smile, she recalled. She would have zapped him with a snappy retort if she'd been the one hurt.

Not wanting to delve into the possibility that Corral's arrogance was a defense mechanism, she welcomed the sight of Sal shouldering the final few lengths of twenty-foot pipe into the building. She parked behind him.

"That's the last of it," Sal called as he dabbed the sweat from his brow with a rag he'd pulled from his back pocket. "Whew-eee. It's hot enough to fry eggs on concrete."

"That it is," she agreed. She hoisted a B-tank to one shoulder, then she trekked toward the building. The temperature would rise another ten degrees shortly after her striker lit the torch. "Thanks for saving me the trouble of hauling the pipe in here."

Sal shoved the damp rag in one pocket and extracted a pen and a folded ticket from another. He held it out for her to sign. "You traded your air-conditioned office in for that?" he teased, pointing to the B-tank.

"Yeah." She set the tank next to the partition where she planned to start. "Temporarily."

"Temporary insanity on your part," he said with a tsking noise. "You know there's a good reason for the crews quittin' at three o'clock. They don't want to fry their brains!"

"Heat doesn't bother me."

Sal chuckled. "You couldn't prove that by me. When I saw you and Corral over yonder, you both looked plenty hot and bothered. Something going on between you two?"

"We were just exchanging pleasantries while I waited for you," she fibbed. She checked the sheets, initialed the last page at the bottom and returned the forms. "Mind putting the pink copy on my dashboard when you leave?"

Sal took the receipt, and her broad hint to hit the road. He gave her a quick salute. "Will do."

After Sal had driven off, Molly settled into the task of replacing the water pipe. First she strung the proper grade of copper through the drilled holes overhead and coupled the lengths, then she began soldering the drops to the lines that eventually would carry hot and cold water to the various fixtures.

Her rhythm became quick and efficient as she performed the tasks of measuring, cutting, fluxing and soldering the pipe. Taking pride in the quality of her work, she wiped each joint to make certain there were no solder "huckleberries" dripping off the copper.

Mindlessly she performed her work, not having to think about what step was next. When her mind began drifting toward her immediate problems, she realized that as a teenager, she'd worried about scores of dilemmas while sitting on a workbench.

In her dreamworld, academic and social success were a snap. The girl who never drew attention to her tall, skinny body by raising her hand in class changed into a petite student who eagerly waved, frantic to share her vast knowledge. She strolled down the hall with the most popular clique of girls, giggling, sharing secrets and flirting with the jocks.

And she had a real boyfriend who worshiped the ground where her dainty feet trod. She dreamed of the day when she'd juggle being a wife and mother with being the driving force behind her father's business.

Since her divorce, she'd been too caught up in the chores of surviving from day to day. Molly blew her bangs out of her eyes as she mentally blew away the ugliness of her marriage. She'd grown beyond classifying all men as a subspecies of the human race that lived under slimy rocks.

I've grown in other ways, too, she reflected. Ashamed of her height, she'd slouched through junior high, high school and her marriage.

Now she held her head high. She'd learned there were advantages to being tall. She often confirmed them by verbalizing them aloud the instant they occurred to her.

"Brandon Corral would be a weather vane by now if I hadn't been able to move the ladder," she murmured.

Just mentioning Corral's name brought out the fighting spirit she'd also acquired. She'd learned submissiveness shrank her self-esteem, not her height.

And yet, in the solitude of her thoughts, she had to admit Corral did frighten her. Not superficially like a bone-chilling horror movie, but on a deeper level. She'd met other men who were shrewd, willing to go to any length to get what they wanted. They hadn't appealed to her.

Why Corral?

The mesmerizing effect Corral had on her senses disturbed her. She should have known from his initial telephone conversation with John that Corral was a man to be reckoned with. Neither John's bluster nor her silent treatment had discouraged Corral. Nor had her most reliable defense mechanism been effective. Once or twice Corral flinched when she hurled a barb at him, but he kept coming back for more.

Undefeatable, persistent and damned attractive. A dangerous combination worthy of any sane woman's fear, she decided. And awe. And respect. And desire?

"Ouch!"

Molly jerked her hand back from the copper she'd inadvertently overheated. The pipe clanged and bounced against the concrete floor. Her heart banged against her ribs. She removed her glove and stuck her finger in her mouth to relieve the tingling sensation. She glanced at the scorched fitting and came foolishly close to tears.

Only a feebleminded ignoramus would *desire* the enemy.

It's you I want, Molly. To hell with Winsome and Corral Plumbing.

Dammit, she scolded silently, desire has no place in an adversarial business relationship.

Why? she questioned. Why now? Why *him?*

Idly, she picked up the flux brush, dabbed it in the flux can and swiped over the black smudge on the pipe. For the next hour Molly made a herculean effort to thrust her desire for Brandon Corral out of her mind by immersing herself in work.

Only when the flare of her torch became the sole source of light did she realize she was losing her race against the clock to complete the job. She'd finished the kitchen and two bathrooms. A half bath and the laundry remained unconnected to the main line.

From outside she heard her name called, once, twice, three times. Each call grew in volume and impatience. She recognized Corral's voice. He must have spotted the red sticker, she figured, and wanted to gloat.

"In here!" she shouted, wishing she'd parked her truck in back of the building, where he could not have seen it.

Brandon passed through a front window opening into what would eventually be the living room. He'd seen the sticker and her truck. Putting one and one together, he'd figured Molly must be correcting whatever minor problem had caused the building to fail its inspection. As he inventoried Molly's tools and equipment, he realized he'd underestimated her problem. A minor problem wouldn't have taken this long to fix.

"Trouble?"

"You asking or offering?" she snapped.

Brandon grinned. "Getting. Maybe you could lend me a red sticker to paste on my forehead."

"That isn't where I'd put it," she replied, not appreciating his joke. When his smile widened and had its usual effect of sabotaging her nervous system, she thought, I'd paste it over your mouth!

Brandon must have read her mind when he advanced on her and said, "If I had one, I'd paste it over your mouth. Now, do I walk the building, or do you tell me what we need to get finished?"

"Sunlight," she lamented drolly. "There's still the half bath and laundry to do."

Scowling, Brandon let out a hiss of frustration. He'd met women who'd expected the moon and stars, but never one who'd asked for the sun. But then, he'd known from the beginning Molly Winsome was not a typical woman. He wouldn't be here if she were.

A thought stirred him into action. "I'll be right back."

Curiosity stopped Molly from making a smart remark. She rose off the crudely built wooden stool and followed him. He strode past John's truck to his own. As well-equipped as John kept his truck, there were no strings of light stored in it. She would have had to waste time going to the warehouse to get them. Were those Corral's intentions?

Brandon climbed in his Suburban, started the engine and put it into four-wheel drive. Nail-filled rubble lay between his truck and the building's foundation.

"What the hell?" he muttered, shifting into low gear. He'd pick nails from his tires later. He tromped the gas pedal. Seconds later his front bumper hung over a low window frame. The entire concrete slab lit up like the Astrodome when he flicked the switch activating the bar of lights on the roof.

"Yes!" Molly shouted in praise of his ingeniousness.

She'd asked the impossible, and damned if he hadn't delivered! As she watched Corral stride toward her, impulsively she wanted to give him a Texas-sized hug. Fearful a hug would lead further, she denied the urge. "Thanks."

"You're welcome." It was ridiculous how much her approval mattered to Brandon. Earning one of her smiles was worth four tires and a dead battery.

A spirit of cooperation he hoped would last beyond the next hour began when Molly invited his help by asking, "Measure and cut? Or flux and solder?"

"Your soldering is a work of art," he complimented her after glancing at the stub-outs protruding from the copper fittings. "I'll cut and measure."

A warm shade of pink blossomed in her cheeks as she ducked her head to remove the tape measure and pipe cutter from the leather pouch slung low on her hips. As she took a deep breath to steady her jangled nerves, the scent of his expensive after-shave teased her senses. He'd moved closer, inside her danger zone.

Without looking up and careful not to touch him, she gave him the tools he'd need. Considering everything she'd accused him of doing, it amazed her that he was here. She yearned to reach up, take his face in her hands and say, "I'm sorry," with heartfelt sincerity.

Before she could act on her impulse, he'd moved the pipe and work stool to the half bath, then knelt to measure the length of pipe she'd need. She sat on the work stool he'd placed beside him.

It's you I want, Molly. To hell with Winsome and Corral Plumbing.

She heard his words clearly in her mind, as though he'd spoken them for the second time. He'd known her for such a short period. Didn't he realize the ramifications of taking such a personal risk?

Brandon twirled the pipe cutter around the copper pipe with ease. "Did your dad teach you how to solder a joint?"

"Uh-huh." In close quarters, his arm brushed against hers. "When I was little, John made toys from pipe. He'd let me help. What about you? Dad mentioned your family is in car sales. How'd you get into this crazy business?"

"My roommate in college worked construction jobs every summer. His father hired me."

"Ummm," she responded, wondering why he'd swelter in the Texas heat when he could have been wheeling and dealing in an air-conditioned car agency.

She glanced sideways at him, imagining how great he'd look in a suit and tie. He'd finished a measurement, reeled the tape and propped his elbow on his knee, with his finger curled over his mouth. From his body language, she knew her curiosity about him getting "a leg up" was not going to be assuaged.

She fluxed a ninety-degree fitting, then assembled it with the stub-out Brandon had cut and a copper cap. Before soldering it in place, she checked to make certain it was plumb with a torpedo level.

"So, you went from toy maker directly to Winsome Plumbing?"

"More or less."

While she soldered, he began fluxing fittings. "I'm not certain I'd want my daughter on a construction site."

"John isn't a male chauvinist."

"Neither am I. But I wouldn't get much work accomplished if I had to follow my daughter around, keeping the horny workers from seducing her."

Amused, Molly laughed. "Tomboys don't get catcalls and whistles. That wasn't a problem, believe me."

He didn't. The look he gave her should have lit the torch she held in her hand. It didn't, but it did thaw her icy reserve. She clicked the striker.

"By nineteen I was married and had moved to Dallas. Two years later I was back in Austin, divorced."

Surprised by her candidness, Brandon sat back on his haunches and studied her face. There were no bitter lines bracketing her lips, nor had he heard tones of regret in her voice. She looked confidently serene as she wiped the joints of pipe.

Enticingly beautiful, he added silently, and unconsciously provocative.

"What about you?" she inquired softly. "Single? Married? Divorced?"

"Single." Giving his reply second thought, he said, "Married."

"And just a little bit pregnant?" Molly teased, glad he hadn't quizzed her about the whys of her failed marriage.

Brandon chuckled. Claiming to be single and married was the same as claiming to be a little bit pregnant. You either are or you aren't. No in-betweens.

"Single but committed to my company," he clarified. On a lighter note he added, "And to saving grown-up tomboys in distress."

"And buying out the competition." The debilitating effect of his smile and tone of voice injected a stab of reality into their conversation.

"Only when they want to sell. I've never forced any man's hand." Or woman's, he added silently. The dark pupils of his eyes had flared, as though inviting her to inspect his soul for black blemishes.

Her eyes met his. She thought she saw sincerity in them, but she'd jumped to too many conclusions to trust her judgment. "You wouldn't take advantage of John being hospitalized to wear down his resistance until he sold Winsome, would you?"

"No."

"Then why were you at the hospital?"

Brandon flinched. Seldom, if ever, did anyone dare to question his conduct. She'd laugh her socks off if she knew why he'd been there. He'd never known love from his grandfather or his father, and yet he'd felt some affinity toward John that he couldn't pinpoint. Stronger than friendship. Stronger than male bonding. Until he'd seen John at the hospital, he'd thought he must have imagined that feeling. He still couldn't put a name to it, and he still couldn't explain it. Automatically his grin became lopsided, cocky.

Flippantly Brandon answered, "I always check up on the men whose lives I save."

Oops, another touchy subject, Molly thought as she watched him run the back of his hand over his lips to seal them. What was he hiding? Ulterior motives?

Was he lying behind his teeth when he said he wouldn't take advantage of John's accident?

While Molly soldered and wiped the last joint in the half bath, Brandon moved behind the kitchen to the laundry room.

She stood, tossing her long braid over her shoulder. Invariably she'd thought the worst of him and had been proven wrong each time. Why did she continue to distrust him?

Because he's a threat, her instincts warned.

How?

He made her feel . . . girlish.

Womanly?

Pretty.

Sexy?

Competent.

Brilliant?

Each time her mind minimized how Brandon made her feel, her heart provided a more accurate assessment. Her heart and mind warred until she felt Brandon's hand on her shoulder.

Flustered at being caught daydreaming, she stammered, "Oh, uh, you're ready?"

"Ready." Willing and able, too, he thought, silently finishing the phrase for her.

"Good." Molly dusted off the seat of her britches while he carried the bench and tank to the laundry room. "We're almost done."

Brandon raised one eyebrow. Not by a long shot, Ms. Molly. We've only just begun.

"I don't know what I'd have done without your help," she said, after he didn't comment. As surely as Brandon had zipped his lips when he'd said more than he'd meant to say, Molly unzipped hers to fill the silence with meaningless chatter. "I would have been here until midnight, stringing lights...and testing the water. My work usually doesn't leak, but I'm not taking any chances. Tomorrow this building will pass inspection."

He set the torch on the floor and turned to her. He stood between her and her work, both physically and emotionally.

"Are you still in love with your ex-husband?" Brandon asked casually.

Molly's mouth fell open and she gaped at him. "Whaaat?"

"I said, are you still in love..."

"I heard you." She squeezed past him and straddled the bench. Her hand trembled as she sorted through the fittings. She drew a shaky breath and replied firmly, "No. Not that it's any of your business."

"Isn't it?"

"No." She flipped her hair out of her eyes. "I'm not looking for a relationship."

Brandon smiled down at her. "Funny, but the nicest things seem to happen when we least expect them."

"Meaning?"

She clamped the striker handles together repeatedly, but the damned thing wouldn't spark. She heard the rake of a matchstick across emery cloth before a small flame held between Brandon's finger lit her torch. He adjusted the flame to prevent her from being singed.

"I wasn't looking, either." He noticed the goose bumps on her forearm when he blew out the match flame and his breath caressed her flesh. "Care to have me prove you wrong?"

"You couldn't." When he leaned closer, she blurted, "Besides, physical attraction is a weak foundation for a lasting relationship."

"Are you speaking from past experience?"

Molly ducked her head, pretending to concentrate on assembling the last fixture. Leon had never turned her body into flame with a casual touch the way Brandon did. In fact, he'd called her an ice maker on the rare days when he was being kind, and a "frigid bitch" in the court deposition for the divorce hearing.

"Ladies don't kiss and tell," she snapped.

Unscathed by the heat in her voice, he trailed his finger down her sensitive nape. He waited until the female adapter was in place, then he crooked her stubborn chin between his thumb and forefinger and gently turned her face toward him. "Is that what you're afraid of, Molly? Of taking a chance on me?"

"I'm not afraid of you." Her knees knocked and her feet trembled in her boots, but she looked him straight in the eye. As he lowered his head and she bravely encircled his shoulders with her arms, she knew she'd eat those false words.

He brushed his lips across hers, as though testing the water, then kissed her a second time, briefly, his lips barely parting, catching her sigh.

It was not what she'd expected. Anticipating a masterful thrust of his tongue, a takeover, a demand for complete submission, she had been set to deny his invasion.

Corporate raiders ruthlessly plundered their prey, didn't they?

Corral's tenderness caught her off guard and unprepared. She could have fought off a physical attack, but not this gentle invasion. His kiss was far sweeter than she would have imagined.

"Now are you afraid?" he asked.

"Yes," she answered bluntly, honestly.

His hand shifted, drifting down each vertebra of her spine until she willingly edged closer to him. His other hand lazily massaged the tension from her shoulders and neck.

"You aren't the only one," he admitted, wary of the feelings she kindled. His instincts warned him that Molly wasn't his usual love-me-and-leave-me-before-dawn woman. Her eyes, bluer than a Texas summer sky, softer than spring rain, beckoned him closer with their shy love-me-forever message. But he had no room in his mind or heart for a woman. Trained to follow his instincts, he should have walked—no, *run*—to the nearest exit.

"I can't imagine you being afraid of any woman." She placed her hand across his chest, feeling the steady rhythm of his heart. It skipped a beat as she molded herself against him. Her fingers advanced and retreated against the warp thread of his plaid shirt.

"You aren't just any woman, Molly. You're different."

What he meant as a compliment, she took as a disparaging remark. She didn't need Corral to tell her she was different. She dropped her arms to her sides.

"And proud of it," she stated flatly. "I can't and won't change. Not for you. Not for him. Not for any man."

The harsh edge of pain he'd heard alerted Brandon. "Him? Meaning your ex-husband? He wanted you to change?"

"Yes." His hand behind her back stalled her attempt to pull away from him. Her eyes shone brighter than blue topaz as she glared up at him. "Doesn't every rich Prince Charming want his Cinderella? My ex tried to make a silk purse from the proverbial sow's ear. He mixed his morality tale." She smiled, but it didn't soften the stoniness of her eyes. "His mother, the queen of Dallas society, should have taught him pigs don't wear size-five glass slippers and real men don't carry a silk purse."

Brandon frowned. Automatically his muscles tightened around her to protect her from her own punch line. He would have given a week's draw to have the man who'd hurt her within punching distance.

"Not funny?"

"Only if Phyllis Diller or Rodney Dangerfield say it." Content with simply holding her, stroking her hair, he broke a cardinal business rule that carried over into his personal life and explained himself. "By different I meant original. Only a fool chooses lithographs or carbon copies or imitations when an original is obtainable. The same idiot would choose a tract house over a custom-built home—brass-plated fixtures over pure brass."

Molly recalled the lithographs hanging in her ex-husband's office and the plated fixtures throughout their home. She smiled warmly. Brandon's words were a balm soothing a raw spot on her soul. She did not love the man she'd hastily married, but she had taken the blame for the marriage failure. Brandon had eased her load, until she felt as light as butane gas. And as dangerously volatile.

When his mouth closed over hers and his tongue teased her lips she felt a fire blazing through her so hotly that it must have radiated heat. She made a sound that crisscrossed between a moan of delight and Brandon's name. The heat and taste of him swept across her tongue. For this short moment in time, she forgot that he was the man who wanted her most prized possession. She forgot everything but the sweet taste of him.

"Say it," Brandon demanded as she kissed his mouth with bewitching delicacy. He sipped her lips and tongue as he wanted to sip at the tips of her breasts. "Not Corral. Say my given name."

"Brandon," she groaned, feeling a fountain of pleasure expanding through her, making her feel wet and wild. "Ahhh, Brandon, what you're doing to me."

"I hope it's a tenth of what you're doing to me," he said urgently, hotly caressing her by alternately peppering kisses and love bites along her neck.

An emotion speared through Brandon the way the headlights of his truck pierced the darkness. He remembered how he'd taken women in the hope of satiating a hunger deep inside him, a pit that sex never filled. With each encounter the pit grew deeper, wider and bottomless, until he believed he would live forever with an empty hole where his heart and soul should have been. Just as taking John by the hand had caused an uncommon stirring of deep emotion, touching Molly had a similar effect, only stronger.

The stool where she sat creaked loudly, tipping toward him.

"I'm sorry," he whispered, brushing her mouth with his teeth, tongue and lips as he ended their kiss. His forehead lazily rocked against hers while he regained his equilibrium. "When we make love, I don't want the bed to be a slab of cold concrete, with sawdust for sheets."

Molly blinked rapidly in an effort to restore her senses. *When we make love,* she repeated silently. She took his hand that rested on her thigh and brushed her lips over the hills and valleys of his knuckles. He'd apologized, without stammering or seeking a means to avoid expressing his sorrow. He wasn't the ruthless man she'd thought him to be. And he wasn't the brash, cocky man she'd come to know.

But she wasn't the woman she'd carefully constructed, either. By hiding behind a computer and a stack of blueprints in the office, she'd avoided men, thus avoiding any change or risking heartache. She'd mentally frozen her sexuality, choosing celibacy to escape her feelings of being gauche and inept in the bedroom. She'd changed.

As she raised her face and their eyes met, she realized both Brandon and her had changed—drastically.

Brandon Corral wasn't her nemesis, but he was an enigma, a heart-shaped puzzle she wanted to solve.

Chapter Six

With unspoken words hanging between them, Molly slowly rose, wondering how to solve the puzzle. Her doubts and reservations about Brandon were mere whispers clamoring against the wild desire coursing through her veins.

"It's too late to test it," Brandon said as he watched her eyes skitter over the pipe. "I'll have one of my men put a hundred pounds of pressure on it in the morning."

His kind offer had the same effect on her fears as air pressure on an unsoldered fitting: they disintegrated.

"Thanks." She glanced at her wristwatch. The headlights of his Suburban had grown dimmer with each passing moment, making it impossible for her to tell time. "Do you think it's too late for us to stop by the hospital?"

Brandon grinned, pleased that she'd included him. "Visiting hours ended at nine. It's close to midnight, Molly."

The bewitching hour, she thought, returning his smile.

"You must be starving by now. I'll pick up a bucket of chicken and you can meet me at my place." He paused, then added, "On second thought, maybe you'd better follow me."

His offer sounded casual, but she could feel the intensity of his eyes as he watched her pack up her tools, preparing to leave. Before she could heave the workbench to her shoulder, Brandon took it.

Amused by his arrogant assumption that she'd follow him, she asked, "Why?"

"Because I don't want you to get lost."

"I know Austin's roads like the back of my hand."

With his free hand, Brandon effortlessly hoisted the B-tank and balanced it on his shoulder. "Good. I'd say, judging from the looks of my headlights, my battery is almost dead. Unless you have some cables..." Watching the dim light dance like flames in her hair as she shook her head, he added, "Guess I'll be riding with you."

Molly chuckled and strode toward her battered truck. While he stashed her tools and B-tank in the bed, she gloated, "Does that mean you're stranded and I have to save you... again?"

"Get in," he ordered, grinning. After he'd retrieved his keys and locked his truck, he said, "I'll drive."

"I'll drive. Old Betsy can be cantankerous," she whispered, as though the truck had ears and was easily offended.

She slid into the driver's seat; Brandon squeezed in beside her.

"Cantankerous women are becoming my specialty," he bragged. Before she could loop her legs across the gearshift, he circled her shoulders with one arm and turned her face toward him with his hand. "Are you going to be difficult?"

"No more than eating soup with a fork," she quipped.

"Or digging a ditch in Lake Travis?" he countered, nibbling the side of her neck.

"Or..." His tongue flicked the small lobe of her ear, making coherent thought nearly impossible, much less a witty comeback. "Or...picking up mercury...with a pair of tweezers."

"Or concentrating on driving with you in my lap," he murmured, nipping the nubbin of flesh he held captive between his teeth.

He detained her from moving across the seat with one long, smoldering kiss. Overwhelmed by his scent, taste and touch, she tingled with pleasure and the desire to have more of him. Her eyes were still closed when he lifted her into the passenger's seat.

"Keys please," he requested, his voice raw and hoarse.

She'd held them so tightly in her hand while she'd kissed him that they'd left an imprint on her palm. She relinquished them without another sassy word.

"Okay, sweet Betsy," Brandon crooned, "be good."

Much to Molly's surprise, when he inserted the key into the ignition, old Betsy came to life and hummed as though she'd recently had a tune-up. No buck-snorts ripping out the tail pipe. No grinding of gears when shifted into reverse.

Amazing. Utterly amazing, Molly thought, wanting Betsy to misbehave.

"Pizza, chicken or Chinese?" Brandon asked.

"Anything is fine." The cheeky grin spreading across his face made her feel that she was as easily controlled as her truck! Perversely, Molly straightened and firmly said, "Burger Doodle."

"That's my girl." He patted the dashboard. "For a moment I thought you were slipping gears."

"Who? Me? Or Betsy?"

"You."

"Which means?"

"You aren't the passive type. You know what you want and you state it plainly."

Molly grinned. She liked the image Brandon had of her: independent, decisive and outspoken. She didn't want him to know she'd spent the first twenty years of her life trying to please her father and the next five years trying to fit the sophisticated image her ex-husband had molded.

Fiercely determined to maintain the impression she'd made on him, when they pulled to a stop at the drive-up window she said, "A cheeseburger. Plain. No mustard or mayonnaise."

"Fries? A Coke?"

Molly nodded to answer both his questions. He leaned through the window to place the order. She had reached forward to tap him on the shoulder and ask for ketchup to go with her fries, when she noticed the black stains on her fingers. The brown cotton gloves she'd worn while working had protected her hands from the greasy flux, but her hands were still a mess.

And so were her clothes, she noted, grimacing at the sawdust clinging to the front creases of her jeans. Discoloration marked the sleeves of her pale blue shirt where she'd wiped sweat from her brow. To put it mildly, she mused with dismay, she looked like something disreputable that the dog had dragged in and the cat refused to touch.

Brandon glanced at her and smiled. "This shouldn't take long."

"I'm going to perpetuate the plumbing trade while we're here."

Before he could yea or nay, Molly was out of the truck, hurrying toward the side door. Within a minute, she stood under the high-wattage bathroom lights, gazing into the mirror. Thoroughly aghast at her appearance, she wondered why Brandon hadn't dumped her off at her house and sped off down the highway.

Without lipstick or a comb, transforming herself from plumber to seductress seemed an impossible task. She turned on the tap and twisted the black handle on the soap dispenser. Powdered grit that closely resembled drywall paste filled her palm. For an instant, she longed for the expensive, perfumed face cream she'd used while living the pampered life in Dallas.

"No, ma'am," she said, wetting her hands and briskly rubbing them together. What good is face cream when you can't look at yourself in the mirror? "The price was too high."

She scrubbed her hands and face, rinsed her mouth, then dried herself on a coarse paper towel. While she tucked stray tendrils of her russet hair into the weave of her French braid, Molly scrutinized her reflection in the mirror.

Not cosmetic perfection, she decided. She felt clean and refreshed. Less critical eyes would have noted that her skin had a healthy glow from working outdoors, and her eyes sparkled with anticipation. But years of being compared with women who spent hours pampering themselves with facials, manicures and massages had made Molly unaware of her own natural beauty.

Brandon wasn't.

He'd watched her graceful, long-legged, slim-hipped saunter across the parking lot, and had to adjust the inside seam of his jeans to accommodate himself. His male hormones had been giving him hell from the first moment he'd caught Molly to keep her from falling. He'd made no bones about wanting her. She'd wanted him, too. He'd seen it in her eyes.

But she'd stubbornly refused both his offers. She wouldn't let the man who'd "pushed" her father from the roof help. She wouldn't consider starting a relationship with the same man who'd made it clear that he wanted to acquire Winsome Plumbing. She'd made both points abundantly clear.

Aroused and furious, he'd silently sworn to let her sink or swim under her own power.

Yet as the day had progressed, he'd found himself making excuses to go back to the South Shore project. He'd wondered what the hell she was doing in that house that took so long? Where the hell were her men? It infuriated him to think she was soldering pipe together all alone. Man's work. Dammit, she was management, not labor!

By late afternoon, he'd rationalized her asking to borrow a few lengths of pipe to a broad generalization: she needed his help. And the hard fact that she considered him remotely responsible for her father's accident had compelled him to take action.

Did she think he was the type of man who could stand by idly and watch a woman struggle to complete a man's job? Granted, she was taller than most men, but he'd held her, felt the delicateness of her bones, the womanly slenderness of her build. She did not want his help, but by damned, she was going to get it.

"Sunlight," he murmured, remembering what she'd told him she did need. The smile she'd given him when he'd positioned the Suburban's headlights had warmed his insides hotter than sunlight could have. Later, when they'd finished the work and he'd kissed her, he'd felt as though he was standing inside a circle of flames.

Remembering that she'd told him she'd been married, he scowled. What wisecrack had she made? Something about creating a silk purse out of a sow's ear and real men not carrying a silk purse? Her ex-husband tried to change her and hadn't liked the results. Thinking back, Brandon recalled her also saying a woman with size-five feet wouldn't have been able to move the ladder the night he'd been stranded on the rooftop.

His fingers coiled and tightened on the steering wheel. The thought of any man verbally abusing Molly made a red haze of anger cloud his vision. Physical abuse caused bruises on the body; verbal abuse wounded the soul.

Molly, Molly, Molly, he commiserated inwardly, I'd cut my tongue out before I'd intentionally hurt you!

"Your order, sir," the waitress said pleasantly. "Two cheeseburgers, fries and colas?"

Lost in his corrosive thoughts, Brandon snapped his attention to the woman holding the sack and drinks outside the drive-up window.

"I, uh, checked the order," she stammered. "Twice. And there's s-s-salt, ketchup and napkins in the bottom of the s-s-sack."

He realized he must have glared ominously at her. A slow smile curved his lips, an unspoken apology, as he said, "Thanks. I appreciate it."

He shifted and pulled the truck forward too soon to hear the girl giggle nervously and loudly declare, "Lordy, lordy... I think I'm in love."

But Molly heard her.

Smiling, she rushed between the tables and out to the awaiting truck. Although she'd only been able to make minor repairs in her appearance, Brandon rewarded her efforts with a smoldering, sensuous look.

Betsy lurched forward and stalled.

"Clutch?"

"Good idea."

He wrapped his fingers around her slender neck, slid them down her spine, then he pulled her into his arms. He slanted his lips across hers, warm and hard.

He'd intended to seal her sassy mouth with a brief peck, but her lips parted slightly, beckoning him to slide his tongue into the sweetness of her mouth; his intentions changed.

Male hunger that he'd held in check while he'd watched her bend and twist and stretch to install the copper pipe unleashed itself. He shuddered and thrust deeply into her, wanting to draw on her sweetness until her arms clung tenaciously around his shoulders. Soft, so soft, and yet he knew he didn't have to worry about crushing her. She made no move to stop him when he inched his hand up her side. Her back arched, and she yielded to his touch as he cupped the rounded fullness of her breast.

Molly almost cried out from the intense pleasure his thumb provoked by slowly, ever so gently, rubbing her lacy bra against the nipple of her breast. His lips moved to the sensitive place at the base of her neck that he'd discovered earlier. The delicate biting kisses detonated a quiet alarm in the back of her mind, warning her to hold back her soft moans of encouragement.

Shhhhh, be quiet!

The only man she'd known intimately had taught her to repress her desires. Nice women didn't feel as though they'd come unsoldered and fall apart. Only bad women, tramps and two-bit sluts caterwauled their demand for sexual fulfillment.

From the dark, secret recesses of her mind, she clearly heard: *A real man wants a reticent woman.*

Her sudden stillness alerted Brandon. "What's wrong?"

"Nothing."

Disbelieving her too-quick reply, Brandon looked down into Molly's face. Her bottom lip trembled; her mouth moved, as though she wanted to retract her reply and give him an honest answer. Her eyelashes lowered and her lips clamped shut. Although her pulse pounded raggedly beneath his hand, her skin felt cool.

"You're right," he said, his voice harsh. Silently he cursed his baffling lack of self-control with her. He'd kissed and pawed her like some randy cowpoke fresh off a three-month cattle drive. "The front seat of a pickup truck isn't any better than a bare concrete floor."

"We could draw an audience," she quipped, pointing out her open window. The teenage girl who thought she'd fallen in love with Brandon at first sight stood at the plate-glass window, peering straight at them. "I wouldn't want to make her jealous."

"Sorry," he murmured, levering himself away from her.

Before she realized what she was doing, her fingers twined into his shirtfront to detain him. She brushed her mouth against his and emitted a long sigh of regret.

"Careful, lady," he teased. "One more of those and I won't care if the neighbors sell raffle tickets to watch us."

Several thoughtful miles down the road, during which neither of them had spoken, the aroma of burgers and fries brought Brandon out of his intro-spection.

"You must be starved, Molly. I know you didn't stop working to eat lunch. Why don't you help yourself to the food?"

"What about you? Can you eat and shift gears?"

He tilted his head back and gave her a you've-got-to-be-kidding look. The steep hills and sharp curves required attention, but any Texan worth his salt could eat with one hand, chug a drink with the other and still manage to reach his destination.

"Of course you can," Molly agreed, being the last person who wanted to offend his masculinity.

Her father seldom drove without having some munchies available and something to wet his whistle. Fries on the dashboard, sandwich in his left hand, drink between his legs—she knew the routine by heart.

No trouble with placement of the fries and cheeseburger, but Brandon had to downshift to second just as she stuck the straw into his drink. He couldn't take the cup and put it between his legs. The dashboard lights dimly lit the cab's interior, but she could see well enough to notice his left thigh contract and extend as he worked the clutch.

What had started as an act of consideration suddenly became intensely intimate.

She swore that it wasn't her fault when her knuckles brushed against the inside seam of his jeans. And it had been absolutely necessary for her to steady the cup when the front wheels swerved to avoid hitting a pothole. Automatically, his muscular legs had clamped around it, almost trapping her hand. Surely there wasn't any doubt in his mind that she had *in-*

tentionally touched the zipper of his fly in her haste to extricate her fingertips, was there?

A sidelong glance at the wicked grin on his face made her want to slug him.

While she ate her sandwich, Molly became mesmerized by the ribbon of asphalt winding between massive slabs of granite. The pungent smell of cedars poured through the truck's open windows. She loved the Hill Country outside of Austin's city limits, where a series of man-made dams had tamed the mighty Colorado River, forming huge reservoirs of water.

As they crossed the Mansfield Dam, moonlight shimmered and danced on the smooth surface of Lake Travis. Miles and miles of limestone and granite stone had purified the muddy Colorado until it ran deep and clear, the same bluish purple as a highly faceted sapphire. At a distance, lights appeared to twinkle like stars from the homes perched on the bluffs.

"Don't put your elbow out the window," Brandon warned as he downshifted and turned right on a road barely wide enough for the truck's wheels. Betsy spit gravel as her wheels swerved, but the tires regained traction in the ruts and slowly began to climb the steep grade. Twigs of low-growing underbrush scraped against the truck's body. When he glanced at Molly and saw her teeth clenched against the jarring motion from the washboard road, he promised, "The view is worth it."

The moment they crested the peak, gravel changed to concrete, and a few seconds later, Brandon braked the truck in a triple-wide carport.

"Ever win at playing king of the hill when you were a kid?" He reached across Molly to open her door. "That's how I felt when I bought this lot."

Molly understood why as she stepped from the truck and crossed to the railing. It took little imagination to pretend the world was at her feet. Looking down, it appeared as though the canopies of century-old oaks formed gigantic stepping-stones down a steep slope, to the edge of a bluff that plummeted several hundred feet into the lake.

"Careful." He used the excuse of her leaning across the rail to fold his arms around her slender waist. Slowly adjusting her backside until it fitted snugly against the cradle of his pelvis, he said, "One Winsome taking a plunge this week was one too many."

She closed her eyes, not wanting to worry about the accident that had led them to being together. Or the job difficulties she'd encountered because of John being hospitalized. From somewhere in the night, she could hear a mockingbird call its lonesome mating tune over the crickets' summer lullaby. Being locked securely in Brandon Corral's arms while he nuzzled the curve of her neck made her woes seem too distant to be of concern.

Without speaking, Brandon neatly tucked her under his arm and walked beside her into the house. Quiet, intimate darkness enveloped them as he closed the door. Layers of shadows created by moonlight filtering through the open weave of the casement fabric drapes was all she could see. She sensed soaring, cathedral ceilings and expanses of glass, but with her arm draped around his solid back, her ear and nose against his chest, she didn't need to see.

She trusted him to know the way as they moved down a long, curved flight of steps. To have switched on the lights would have broken the intimate spell being woven around her. They had reached the last step, when Brandon turned, keeping one foot on the step as he wrapped his arms around her waist, lifting her against him, then lazily let her slide against him until her toes barely touched the carpet.

Face upturned, she hungrily awaited his kiss.

Hesitating, Brandon framed her face with his hand, wanting to give her a last chance to change her mind. Although the tremendous self-control his mind had over his body clung by a bare thread, he desperately wanted this to be right for both of them.

"Brandon?"

"Mmmmm?"

She covered his hand with hers, coaxing it down her throat, where her pulse fluttered wildly, down the hollow of her collarbone, down the fullness of her breast, until his hand covered her heart.

He felt her quiver beneath his touch. He could have made her beg him to make love to her. She would have eventually, just as she'd had to ask to borrow supplies from him. But he hadn't needed to hear her plead then any more than he needed to hear her plead now. He'd give what she wanted, needed, because his own need had always been greater than hers.

He slanted his mouth across hers, hungry, greedy, demanding she accept the thrust of his tongue. His foot still on the step, he nudged his knee between her legs, parting them until she straddled his thigh. Bent at the waist, he pinned her securely between the wall of his chest and his leg while his hands roamed freely up and down her back.

Tall and slender, Molly fitted perfectly against him, and yet the unusual position made her feel tiny, almost petite. When his strong hands began massaging her, causing her to rock intimately against his leg, she kissed him harder and swallowed a small gasp. Each stroke created such a sweet swirling inside her that she could hardly catch her breath.

She wasn't the only one aroused; she could feel the hard ridge of hot flesh beneath his fly. The swirling sensations intensified as she imagined that same rigid muscle moving inside her. She reached down and pressed her hand to him, then lower, to the base of the zipper.

She shouldn't have compared him with her ex-husband, but the difference in size amazed her. Brandon was huge. He bulged against her fingers, as hard and thick as the hickory handle of a carpenter's hammer. He moaned deep in his throat when she unbuttoned the fly; tooth by tooth her fingers ascended the thick zipper.

His mouth left hers briefly, only long enough to urge, "Touch me."

At the same moment, she felt her shirttail being jerked from her jeans. Her hand hadn't climbed an inch, when she felt her bra unhook. Then his hand was inside her shirt and under her lacy bra, cupping her breast.

"Do it, Molly."

A shiver down her spine made her fingers tremble. She fumbled with the brass zipper tab, driving him wild with anticipation. In the best of circumstances, it would not have been easy to draw the tab down the stretched zipper. Finally, the tautness worked to her advantage, and yet she still couldn't touch him. The cotton material of his briefs prevented her from curling her fingers around him.

He must have realized it was impossible, because his foot moved off the step and his leg straightened, removing her support. Molly hadn't realized how greatly he'd affected her until her knees refused to lock. His powerful arm encircled her waist to support her; otherwise she'd have fallen.

He reached behind her legs and lifted her, effortlessly carrying her to his bed. Again she did the unthinkable—she remembered the ghastly incident when Leon had tried to carry her, fireman fashion, and they'd toppled to the floor. A few fumbles later, her ex had railed at her because he'd been "emasculated," unable to perform sexually.

Brandon eased Molly to the satin bedspread. With his arms braced by her shoulders, he watched the emotions flash across Molly's mobile face—a hint of a smile, a slight frown, a scowl. He couldn't read her thoughts, but he intuitively sensed a fleeting memory had crossed her mind.

Of what? he wondered. Another time? Another bed? Another man? His curiosity took a back seat to his driving need as he began stripping off his clothes.

Molly wouldn't allow ghosts from her past to haunt Brandon's bed; she exorcised the demons by wantonly raising her arms in supplication and mouthing Brandon's name.

He smoothed her hair back from her face while he sank next to her on the bed. Returning her slight smile, he started unbuttoning her shirt and said, "One of us is overdressed."

Fascinated, she'd watched him remove his clothing. It occurred to her that she should have been doing the same. Now she was glad she hadn't, because she liked the abrasive strokes his knuckles made against her skin as he teased each button from its hole. And because she could touch what she hotly devoured with her eyes.

Her hands skimmed across his shoulders and arms. He had the awesome strength of a weight lifter, and yet none of the bulk. No unsightly ridge of muscles between his neck and shoulders marred his perfection. Her fingers combed through his dark thicket of chest hair, down the taut muscles of his belly, around to his back and buttocks.

With a shrug of her shoulders and a lift of her hips he'd undressed her, allowing every nerve ending that led to her fevered skin to incinerate against him. Their arms and legs tangled. Wild kisses, short and sharp, marked each newly discovered mound and crevice. She wanted to scream when he fastened his mouth on her breast, fluttering his tongue across her nipple, then sucking hard.

Hot. Wet. Aching for his touch, her legs parted. Her back arched in entreaty. She nudged his hand off the curve of her hip. His hand settled against the hollow of her stomach, seeming to measure the width between her hips. His small finger teased the nest of mahogany hair with feather-light touches, while his tongue continued to circle one dark areola, driving her crazy with desire.

Lower, she silently begged, digging her heels into the soft mattress, rising up to lower his hand. Swallowing convulsively, she writhed and bucked while she held back the command for him to stop teasing her.

As though he'd heard her body shouting at him, the heel of his hand pivoted. He parted the delicate folds of her femininity with his callused fingertips. He dipped into the moist hollow of her woman's body, stroking, rubbing, coaxing, exciting her until he felt the nubbin beneath his palm pulsate against him.

Never had she felt so out of control. She sank her teeth into her lower lip to hold back her moans. Her toes curled, causing the muscles in her legs to bunch. She hadn't noticed he'd held his lower body away from her until she mindlessly hooked her legs against the backs of his thighs to pull him closer.

Willingly, oh so willingly, he moved over her. Holding her hips, he kept himself poised momentarily, then drove fully into her with one powerful thrust. When she wrapped her legs tighter around him and took all of him, he groaned with pleasure. She fitted him as though she'd been created for his special needs.

"All woman," he murmured raggedly, guiding her hips until she undulated against him as he rose to his knees, "liquid fire, consuming heat, pulsating, holding me deep inside you."

Her eyes were squeezed shut, as if to block out everything other than the exquisite feelings from within, but she heard each glorious word of praise he spoke. Her hands clenched the sheets, twisting them into a tight knot as he slowly withdrew, then took her again, increasing the tempo of his thrusts, faster, harder, until sparks ignited in her mind.

She heard his name screamed, echoed by her own.

But she must have imagined them and the fierce explosions ricocheting through her bloodstream. Nothing on earth this magnificent could be real.

Could it?

Each labored breath she took brought her closer to reality. Brandon sprawled on top of her, motionless. Her fingers pushed through his damp hair, touching his scalp, as though giving him soothing caresses would revive him.

Brandon shifted to his side. His eyelids seemed weighted. Through a dark fringe of lashes, he looked closely at Molly. What he saw brought a lazy smile to his lips. The first time with a woman, every man worth his salt wanted to know if it was good for her. The look of wonder and amazement on Molly's face made the manly question seem gauche.

His small smile dazzled Molly, almost as much as what he said.

"You're fantastic . . . the perfect woman."

Chapter Seven

Groggily sitting up in bed, Molly stretched, shaking her tangled hair off her face and luxuriating in the bright sunshine coming through the wall of glass at the foot of the bed.

"Brandon?" she called, her eyes opening wide in alarm as she glanced at her wristwatch. Eight o'clock! She was supposed to be at the warehouse an hour ago. Frantically, she searched the bedroom for the clothes she'd worn yesterday, to no avail. "Brandon!"

She jerked the sheet off the bed. As she wrapped it around herself, she wondered where Brandon had gone. He shouldn't have let her oversleep. She had work to do.

First she had to make certain Yolanda called in for a reinspection. She gathered up the ends of the sheet and charged up the steps two at a time. She followed her nose to the source of the heavenly aroma of brewed coffee. She saw the note propped on the telephone beside the coffee maker and smiled:

> Sweetheart,
> Don't worry. Go back to bed. I'll take care of business. Make yourself at home. Your clothes are in the dryer. I'll be back before dark.
>
> Brandon

She read it a second time, trying to squeeze imaginary love words between the lines. Shaking the page, she thought, scratch out the salutation and this could have been a business memo. Disappointed, she wadded the impersonal note and tossed it into the trash can.

Conceited fool! One night of glorious sex was supposed to transform her into a lady of leisure? Doing nothing? Dependent upon him?

She'd been there—and hated it.

Nobody was going to attend to her business other than Molly Winsome!

A mental picture of Corral sitting in her father's swivel chair, with his feet propped up on her father's desk, had her punching numbers rapidly into the phone.

"Good morning. Winsome Plumbing."

"It's Molly. Put me through to Yolanda," she ordered Stephanie, the receptionist, skipping the niceties.

"I can't. She's on line two with the supplier. I suppose you could talk to Mr. Corral, but he's awfully busy."

Molly fought the urge to scream. How many times had she called Leon's office and received a similar response from her ex-husband's secretary? Dammit, this wasn't Brandon's receptionist; it was hers!

"Busy doing what?" Molly demanded.

"He made several phone calls."

"To?"

"Who knows? He didn't ask me to dial the numbers. I just noticed the light blinking when he put somebody on hold."

"Where is Corral now?"

"He left your office with a bunch of computer printouts and went into the warehouse."

"Printouts!" Molly squawked. She couldn't do anything about Brandon being at Winsome Plumbing, but she hoped he hadn't gained access to her computer. Without the notes she'd typed into the computer yesterday, he'd be as lost as she'd been when she'd seen the blank pages on John's clipboards. "Who gave him the computer's password?"

"The same person who gave him the keys to your truck and the office?"

Molly felt her cheeks turn a guilty red. "I loaned him my truck."

"Oh?" Stephanie giggled nervously. "Well, Yolanda didn't give him the password. She was gonna call the cops...until he took her in your office and sweet-talked her."

"Sweet-talked?"

"I sort of watched them through the hall window."

"You eavesdropped."

"Uh-uh. I couldn't hear what was said. But both of them smiled a lot. She's been running back and forth between offices ever since then."

Molly frowned. Yolanda seldom smiled and refused to run errands. "Brandon must have really laid on the charm."

"Just between you and me," Stephanie drawled softly, "I'd say he could charm the air right out of a woman's tires. Know what I mean?"

Or a woman into his bed, Molly translated, nodding in agreement.

"Don't let him know I've called," Molly instructed briskly. "I'll get there as soon as I can. Got that?"

"But Mr. Corral said you weren't coming in today."

Molly thumped the kitchen counter with her fist. "Who's the boss around there? Me or Corral?"

"You," Stephanie replied meekly. "But..."

Molly tightened the knot in the sheet, wishing it were a noose around Brandon Corral's neck.

"It'll be your butt if you tell him I'm on my way," Molly warned.

"Where are you?"

Molly cleared her throat to stall for time. Telling Stephanie she was at Corral's lake house would be like hooking a water hose to a fire hydrant—gossip would spray everywhere.

"'Scuse me," she said, deciding to ignore the question. "I had a frog in my throat. I'll be there shortly. Please do your best to keep Corral out of my office, would you?"

"Yes, ma'am."

"Bye, Stephanie."

Molly hung up the phone knowing she'd asked the impossible. Stephanie couldn't stop Corral from nosing around in her computer files.

No one could stop Brandon Corral—her included!

She started to pick up the receiver to call the hospital, but the thought of her father asking how things were going brought tears to her eyes.

She'd let her father down again.

The last time he was in the hospital, she'd been in Dallas playing "lady of the manor" with her ex-husband. This time, she was God knows where, with John's fiercest competitor!

Naked.

Without wheels!

How could she tell John that while she'd been sound asleep in Corral's bed, that two-legged snake had slithered out of the house and stolen her truck, not to mention her clothes? How could she admit she'd given Corral the keys to the company's truck and office?

Molly didn't know what hurt her pride the most—falling for Corral or disappointing her father.

"Damn your lousy, stinking hide, Corral. Before I let you win that bet, I'll nail that brand-new carpenter's belt to your forehead. Even if I have to walk ten miles naked through the heart of downtown Austin to do it!"

Frowning, Brandon glanced from the computer screen to the familiar picture of Molly and John standing in front of Winsome Plumbing's warehouse. Whoever had taken the picture had captured the sparkle of intelligence in Molly's eyes, and the stubborn tilt of her chin. Wind caught her long, naturally curly hair, pushing it back from her face. He knew it felt like raw silk and smelled of shampoo. Just as he knew how every square inch of her felt and smelled.

And tasted, he thought. Thoroughly captivated by the thought of her curled up, sleeping soundly in his bed, he smiled.

His bed. His woman.

His!

Brandon had never considered any woman as *his*. Truth be known, he avoided energy-draining emotional entanglements. Strange, but their night of lovemaking had increased his energy level. At four o'clock, he'd awakened. After leisurely making love to her, he'd left the lake house feeling as though he could slay at least two or three corporate dragons before breakfast.

His smile widened. The dragon lady who'd tried to scorch his socks earlier entered the room.

"Yes, Yolanda?"

"The supply truck is out front." She held several pages of pink slips out for his signature. "The driver wouldn't let me initial these because they're billed to Corral Plumbing. Why?"

"Expediency," Brand replied, smiling.

"I checked the prices." She raised one eyebrow skeptically. "How come they're lower?"

Brand scribbled his initials on the bottom of each page. "Volume purchases. The bigger the order, the bigger the discount."

"Molly only orders what we need. She'll have a hissy-fit when she sees what you've done," Yolanda threatened.

"I'll take care of Molly."

Yolanda snorted indelicately. "So you've said."

"Here you go." Brand hesitated before he returned the invoice slips. "Who usually checks the delivery?"

"John."

"In that case, I'd better get out to the warehouse." He followed Yolanda through the door. "Have Stephanie direct my calls to the warehouse."

"When did you say Molly would be here?"

Chuckling, Brandon answered, "You can't believe she's taking the day off, can you?"

"Uh-uh, I can't. Molly is the first one here and the last to leave. She hasn't taken a day off since she came back from Dallas."

"Well then, a day or two of vacation won't hurt her, will it?"

Yolanda shook her head and said, "She's been on a guilt trip since the last time John had health problems. I hope you aren't packing her bags for another one."

Parting ways on a semisour note, Molly's secretary returned to her office and Brandon strode into the warehouse.

The delivery-truck driver stopped stocking the empty bins with copper fittings, shooting him a grin. "Hey, Mr. Corral, you taken over here, too?"

Before Brandon could answer, he heard Molly reply.

"Over my dead body." She stepped from behind the boxes that had been unloaded from the truck. "Thanks for the help. I'll finish stocking up."

Both men stood rooted to the spot. She was looking at the driver, but Brandon sensed he himself had been summarily dismissed. When she turned toward him, her eyed blazed with challenge.

That dog don't hunt, he thought, his eyes narrowing as she struggled to heft a carton to her shoulder. He crossed the distance between them and grabbed for the box.

"I can do this," she said fiercely, her tone barely above a whisper.

"Yeah, you can, but not while I'm standing around empty-handed."

Unwilling to create a scene in front of a man who made the rounds to all the local plumbing companies, she relinquished her hold. Her glance swept over the mountain of boxes and pipe she hadn't ordered. As it was, the deliveryman had plenty to tell.

Not willing to take no for an answer, she said to Brandon, "I'll unload the small boxes."

"Fine." His forced smile told her otherwise. "Where do you want the cartons stacked?"

"To the back, on your left," the driver replied, edging toward the door but trying not to make it appear as though he was retreating hastily. "See y'all."

Seconds after she heard the truck depart, Molly dropped the box she carried and whirled around. "Just what the hell do you think you're doing ordering all these supplies?"

"You can't operate a business without materials." His smile didn't waver as he inspected her from her sassy ponytail to her boots, but he wondered where he'd gone wrong. "This should keep you well-stocked until the end of the month."

"*Over*stocked," she snapped, wondering how in the world she was going to juggle the monthly draw from the general contractor to cover the supply bill and the payroll.

"I put them on my account," Brandon informed her, hoping it would erase the worried frown from her face.

"You what?" she exploded.

Brandon lifted another box. His motions were jerky, as though he felt ill at ease with the knowledge that he'd shown a tasteless display of affluence. Or it could have been that he wanted a solid object between Molly and him for protection. She was rubbing her hands down the outside seams of her jeans as though her hands were itching to slap him silly.

She stalked after him as he turned and strode to a darkened corner of the warehouse, where he stacked the next box.

"I told you that I don't need your help," she spit.

"I promised your father—"

"I absolve you from your promise!"

"I told him I'd take care of his business."

"Winsome Plumbing is *my* responsibility!"

Brandon moved around her, continuing to do the heavy work. She lunged for his elbow before he could pick up another box. He spun around, catching her off balance, and pulled her roughly into his arms. He buried his face against the vulnerable place on her throat where her pulse fluttered wildly.

"Molly, Molly, Molly," he soughed, punctuating her name with sharp, brief kisses along her neck.

Thrilling to his touch, she felt her throat working as she tried to summon a command for him to stop.

"You stole my clothes, my truck...and now you're..."

"Stealing your heart?"

He lifted his head at the same moment hers tilted upward. Their mouths sought each other. Kindled by passion, their kiss was desperate with desire. When she would have ended it too soon, he plowed all ten fingers into her upswept hair and held her head while he made love to her open mouth with his tongue.

"I had a helluva time leaving my bed this morning. That's never happened to me," he admitted. "I wanted to make love with you again and again. I wanted you there when I came home. I looked forward to quitting early to be with you."

"No," she protested as a sense of déjà vu caused her arms to drop to her sides. She'd been a rich man's toy, a useless plaything. And while she'd been bored stiff, her father had been too proud and sick to let her know how much the business needed her. Her eyes evoked her pain as she said, "I have to work."

"I'll do it." He freed his hand to loop her arms around him. "Later."

"I can't let my father down. He needs me."

"I need you." He ground his hips against her explicitly.

"You are our competitor. I can't let you..."

His finger followed the vee of her shirt's lapel. He could feel her heart racing, pounding as hard as his own. "Can't? Or won't?"

"Both. Neither."

His callused fingertips caused her confusion. She wanted him; she wanted to be independent. She needed to be needed, but in more than a physical sense. And she had to prove to herself she could be self-sufficient, not a mere shadow cast behind the man she loved.

Brandon tilted her head back and pierced her with a dark stare. "Do you want me to leave?"

No! She wanted him to stay. Wisps of her hair clung to his fingers as he untangled them from her hair. Her throat constricted with emotion. She couldn't squeeze a word past the lump lodged there.

She could only nod.

He stepped back, which forced her to stand on her own without his support. Starkly, with double meaning, he said, "Call me if you need me."

He pivoted on his heel and strode toward her office, not giving a backward glance. Molly watched, her teeth clamped to keep herself from calling out to him.

As he paced the length of the hallway to her office, every killer instinct he possessed told him Winsome Plumbing was ripe for the picking. The company was undercapitalized and strung out between general contractors, and all it would take for them to belly up financially would be for one of their men to spill a gallon of purple primer.

He stared hard at the wall of glass separating Molly's office from the hallway, concentrating on thinking of her as a businesswoman instead of the warm, willing woman he'd held in his arms.

Yeah, maybe the hurt rumbling in his gut had caused him to exaggerate her financial picture, but not by much. Winsome Plumbing's reputation for doing good work at low prices would allow her to continue to rob Peter to pay Paul for a while.

For at least as long as the building boom lasted, he stipulated silently. Eventually Peter and Paul—hypothetical names for the plumbing suppliers—would nail Winsome's doors closed. After all, suppliers were in business for the bucks. Right now, the suppliers were satisfied with the pay-as-you-go status of Winsome's account. Undoubtedly they jacked up the prices for material, lowering the profit margin for Winsome, which only allowed the plumbing company to struggle along at subsistence level. Once Winsome's cash flow slowed, those same suppliers would flush the company down the tube without an ounce of remorse.

He gathered the paperwork he'd brought from his office into a pile. The printouts from her computer verifying his suspicions were next to his briefcase. His hand lingered over them, but he didn't touch them.

There's no room for sentimentality in business. Brandon's grandfather had drummed that into his head since he was a youngster. *Missing an opportunity is like falling off a wagon; you have to walk home when you could have rode.*

Jake Corral practiced what he preached. When other car dealerships floundered, he'd bought them at bargain-basement prices. People who missed payments on cars he'd financed soon missed their vehicles. Mercilessly, during the worst years of the eighties recession, the old man had driven a repo truck himself!

Brandon massaged the back of his neck, where a dull pain had begun to throb. He'd be doing Molly a favor to buy out her father, he rationalized. Why work from dawn to dark for a pittance when the final outcome was inevitable? Wasn't selling out to him preferable to going bankrupt? John could retire at the lake with his buddies and Molly would...

Hate him!

The prospect of her reaction made him feel sick. His dark brows tugged together above his worried eyes. He'd be a sentimental fool to pass up this chance to expand his operation, to be the number-one plumbing contractor in central Texas. He'd worked long and hard to reach that goal.

He glared at the glossy picture framed on her desk. He wished like hell John had never fallen off that damned roof, that he himself had never gotten to know John or Molly. Especially Molly. She distracted him from his goals and tied his stomach in knots.

Reaching into his slacks pocket, he pulled out her keys and dropped them on her desk.

She wanted to run Winsome Plumbing? Let her want!

He'd given his word.

A man didn't go back on his promises!

He shoved the printouts into his briefcase. With Corral Plumbing's purchasing power, he could pound down the prices the suppliers charged her. Maybe get her credit extended.

The booty he'd pirated from her computer would help save Winsome Plumbing, whether she liked it or not.

Chapter Eight

"He only wants to help," John argued, scowling fiercely at his daughter.

Kate stepped to the side of the bed. "Don't excite him, Molly. And as for you, John Winsome... If you keep scrounging around in the bed, I'll tie you down!"

"You'll have to wait until Molly leaves," he mumbled into her ear as she bent over him to fluff his pillow. "You can be on top, too."

Molly bit her tongue to keep back the lengthy list of sins Brandon Corral had committed.

Nor did she want to reveal her own foibles.

She'd had no concept of how difficult the job of riding boss could be. The rash of red stickers on their pipe from the plumbing inspectors was epidemic. While she'd hustled from job site to job site, repairing the mistakes she'd overlooked, Corral had been busy, as well.

Upon Molly's return to the office, Yolanda had smirked and handed her a stack of telephone messages from suppliers and builders. Before she'd read the first one, Stephanie buzzed through. Mark Hanson, chief plumbing inspector, was on the line.

"Just the man I want to talk to," she'd huffed with indignation. "Damned nitpicker!"

The receiver was barely to her ear, when she heard Mr. Hanson say, "Sorry to hear about your father's accident, Molly. I've instructed my men to give you a call before they red-tag anything. Of course everything has to meet code, but under the circumstances I think we can cut you a little slack."

Her eyebrows shot toward her hairline. "Hard-nosed" Hanson was giving her a break? There was a rotten smell on the East wind breeze—and it wasn't caused by the Danish eating Limburger cheese.

She smothered the bile rising in back of her throat with a coat of sugar sweetness and asked, "Perchance, did Mr. Corral contact you?"

"Come to think of it, I do believe it was Brandon who mentioned your father's unfortunate accident. Can't imagine why, but that young man said he held himself responsible. Good man, Brandon Corral."

"Most excellent," Molly quipped, silently seething. How dare Corral ask the plumbing department for favors on her behalf! "I appreciate your call, but I have everything under control."

"It's business as usual?" Hanson asked skeptically.

"Absolutely."

For her ingratitude, the next five minutes she'd had to listen to a list of minor code violations. Her ears had burned when she'd hung up the phone.

Then Stephanie had barged into her office to quiz her about "that gorgeous man with those sexy, bedroom eyes." Molly had impolitely shooed the receptionist out the door, then read the telephone messages.

Why, she'd wondered, were several suppliers she'd never done business with suddenly offering her a line of credit? Curiosity got the best of her.

She'd returned the calls. It didn't take a mathematician to figure out what had caused the splurge of generosity. One good customer strong-arming several suppliers equaled each supplier extending credit to Winsome Plumbing.

They could take their credit and jettison it through a six-inch PVC pipe! She'd pay cash. No interest. No late charges. If she didn't have the money in the bank to cover a check, Winsome Plumbing couldn't afford it.

On her way out the door, Yolanda had informed her that the sheets Corral had printed out were mysteriously missing.

Mysterious, my size-eleven foot! Molly knew exactly who had them and where they were: Corral Plumbing. Both women swore on a stack of Bibles that they hadn't given Corral the password.

She hadn't believed either of them, until she'd spoken to her father.

After hemming and hawing, John admitted that he had been the one who'd given Brandon Corral the code word!

Had her father suffered more than a mild concussion? Had he lost his mind? Had the fall damaged his common sense?

Those thoughts crossed her mind as she sat beside the hospital bed, watching John squirm. She'd been tight-lipped about the other problems she'd wrestled with all day. The censorious glance Kate hurled made Molly flinch.

Who was she to throw stones? John would have every right to toss boulders at her if she told him where she'd awakened this morning.

"I'm sorry I upset you, Dad," Molly apologized. "I'm certain no harm has been done."

John chuckled, grabbed his ribs and coughed. He pointed to the western novel on the bedstand. "Reminds me of the story I'm reading. It's about a renegade Indian named Lone Wolf, who sets off with a war party to raid an army fort."

He gestured for Kate to show it to Molly. On the cover, a man stripped to the waist, his buckskin britches straining at the seams, rode a galloping horse.

"The hero saves a blue-eyed, pale-skin woman. She's been snake-bitten."

"What does this book have to do with Brandon helping Molly?" Perplexed, Kate fanned through the pages of the book. "Or you giving him the password?"

"Be patient, Kate, I'm getting to the point. You see, Molly, I figure Brandon must have the same code of honor as the good guy in this book. Save a life—you're responsible for it."

"Let me guess," Molly said dryly. "Brandon gave you the book, right?"

John grinned. "Matter-of-fact, he did. I'm just to the good part, where Lone Wolf finds out the woman he saved is the daughter of the fort's commander."

"Undoubtedly she's fallen madly in love with the hero?" Kate returned the book to the nightstand. When he nodded, she gave her husband a tender smile of approval. "More men should read romances."

"Wouldn't hurt a certain young lady I know, either," John grumbled. "Just because she's been snake-bitten doesn't mean all men slither on their bellies."

Kate redirected her smile to include her daughter. "Don't hassle her, John. You give our girl a job, and you can depend on her to get it done."

"Thanks, Mom," Molly muttered, needing the verbal pat on the head.

John yawned. "Everything is going okay?"

"On schedule," Molly fibbed. No need to worry a bedridden man, she justified. Before he could catch his breath to ask specific questions, she bent over and kissed his forehead. "You rest. I'll see you tomorrow."

Kate walked her to the corridor. "Try to get an early night, would you?"

"Yeah. You, too."

A mischievous glint twinkled in her mother's eyes as she replied, "I shouldn't admit this, but I sort of enjoy having your father's undivided attention."

Brandon rubbed his hands together in anticipation. She'd call him, he mused confidently. How could she ignore his meddling? Help, he corrected. Meddling had a negative connotation. Everything he'd done was good.

He sat in front of the blank television screen waiting for the phone to ring. Smiling, he tried to imagine her words of gratitude but came up short. More than once she'd told him to mind his own business.

Molly Winsome was the most self-reliant woman he'd ever run across. Tenacious and proud and courageous. She was also the most desirable, passionate woman he'd ever met.

From that sassy twitch of copper-colored ponytail to the tips of her emu boots, she was one fascinating female. He liked the challenge he saw in her blue eyes. Her spunk. How those long, shapely legs of hers could match his stride, step for step, never letting him get ahead of her. And he positively loved the way they'd wrapped around him, holding him deep within her.

She was as refreshing as a long drink of Texas springwater.

It amazed him that Molly had no idea how feminine and desirable she was. She was too busy proving she could carry her share of the business load to realize being a woman in a man's domain was a plus she could use.

Hell, one flutter of those inch-long curly eyelashes and the inspectors would be bumbling all over themselves to paste green stickers on Winsome's work.

He chuckled. Molly would grab the inspector by the scruff of the neck and give him a good shake long before it would occur to her to use her well-stocked arsenal of feminine wiles.

His Molly.

He glanced at the phone, willing it to ring. The silence unnerved him. In the course of the past half an hour, his thoughts had his jeans uncomfortably tight. Thinking of her prompted an acute physical response.

He could call her.

Adjusting his fly, he shook his head. What was the old saying? All good things come to those who... wait? That contradicted every principle Jake Corral had taught him.

Do it. Now. That was his creed for success.

Short on patience, Brandon decided he'd give her another fifteen minutes to call him. By then, visiting hours at the hospital would be over. He settled back in the recliner, kicked off his shoes and unbuttoned his shirt.

Brandon drifted off to sleep, waiting for Molly's call.

Betsy chugged up the steep grade. Downshifting, Molly bit her bottom lip. She'd left the hospital determined to set Brandon Corral straight on who was running Winsome Plumbing.

During the drive to the lake house, she'd changed her mind.

What her father had said about Lone Wolf's code of ethics had heavily influenced her decision. Corral had saved John. Maybe his good deed canceled his nefarious plan to take over Winsome Plumbing by any means.

She was going to give Corral the benefit of the doubt.

And she wasn't going to be sidetracked by physical attraction. Last night had been . . . she grinned impishly, substituting *glorious* for *a mistake*.

She parked behind Corral's fancy Suburban. There was space beside it, but she wasn't taking any chances on his leaving before she did. Chuckling, she shook her head as she admitted her motive for seeing Corral wasn't completely business related.

On a personal level, she had to make him come to grips with the fact that she wasn't a fragile, hothouse petunia. She had her own code: the Texas plumbing code. Factual, not fictional. And she could recite it by heart.

Sliding her keys into her pocket, she crossed to the side entry. She noticed the living-room lights were on and debated whether she should knock. Deciding their spending the night together precluded the courtesy of knocking to announce her arrival, she opened the door and quietly climbed the stairs.

Molly didn't make a sound when she saw Corral asleep. Because he was such a tall man, his ankles and feet hung over the end of the recliner. Barefoot and bare chested, she noticed. Feeling the air-conditioned chill in the room, she went to the sofa and picked up a large, woolly afghan.

The confrontation she planned was the last thing on her mind as she gently spread the afghan over him. His toes moved ever so slightly, but she didn't think she woke him.

Brandon had been wide-awake the second he heard Betsy pull up the drive. He'd heard Molly's boots scrape the steps, the swish of denim on denim as she'd crossed to his side, and caught the faint scent of her hair as she'd fussed over him.

Her hands were as tough as leather from hard work; they felt as soft as velvet when she touched his skin as she tucked the blanket around him. Her simple act of thoughtfulness made his heart smile.

When she turned to leave him, the small pleasure she'd afforded made him too sluggish to snag her wrist. Instead he contented himself to watch her through parted lashes.

Lord, she was beautiful.

Molly stopped beside his desk; the computer printouts caught her attention. She didn't have to sit down and pore over the columns again and again to know what the bottom tally was. He couldn't make the damned numbers add up to a fifteen percent profit, either. Undoubtedly, from the numbers Corral had circled, they'd both come to the same conclusion. With luck and good weather, Winsome Plumbing would scrape by.

Barely, she mused. The numbers didn't lie, but she felt dismal knowing he'd seen them. Her proud posture sagged.

Didn't he realize he was part of the problem? She had to recount every foot of pipe, every fitting, every pot of primer, to undercut his bids.

She brushed back her hair, which had fallen forward as she'd examined the numbers he'd marked. Earlier she'd examined the purchase orders he'd left on her desk. Volume discounts provided Corral with an edge she didn't have. The more Corral Plumbing expanded, the tighter her profits were squeezed.

She knew it; he did, too.

She had to be strong. Where there was a will, there was a way. Dammit, she'd find it.

She glanced over her shoulder to where Corral slept. How she wished she could allow herself to lean on him and let him share her burden. She didn't dare. Corral was the problem, not the solution. He was too...noble? Her thoughts stumbled on the word, but it fitted him. Yes, he was too noble to take advantage of John being hospitalized.

Against her will, he'd helped her.

It wouldn't be fair for her to ask him to up his bids. Or legal, for that matter. Price-fixing was illegal. Neither company would survive if the owners were behind bars.

Besides, Brandon had done enough for them. After he'd helped get medical assistance for John, he could have walked away guilt free. Flowers, books and stocked shelves in the warehouse were above and beyond the call of duty.

She took back her wish. It was wrong to want him to share her burden. She had to stand on her own two feet. Winsome Plumbing was her responsibility.

Hers alone.

That's what she wanted, wasn't it? To prove to herself, her father and the whole world that she was capable of running the business?

So deep in thought was she that she nearly jumped out of her skin when Brandon's arms stole around her waist. Her heart felt jump-started as it pounded furiously when the flat of his hand moved down her hip, across her taut stomach.

"Still mad at me?" he whispered, nuzzling her hair back behind her ear.

"Furious." With myself, she added silently, wrapping her arms across his.

"Do I owe you an apology?"

"Just one."

As her hips snuggled against him, he groaned. "I should have stayed with you this morning."

"Yesssss." A hiss of pleasure strung through her lips. He'd lifted one hand to cup her breast. His thumb toyed with her nipple playfully. His teeth worried the vulnerable place on her neck.

"And waited to ask you for the password?"

She took a deep breath, willing the fuzziness in her mind to subside. "Yes."

"Would you have given it to me?"

"No."

Abruptly, he turned her until she faced him. "I'm not sorry, Molly."

Bemused, slightly dizzy, she tilted her head to look at his eyes. He was several inches taller than her, and she never seemed to get used to his size. What she saw in his eyes was familiar: impatience, irritation and... beauty. This close, the golden glints dominated his dark brown irises.

"Have you ever been?"

"What? Sorry?"

"Yes."

Pausing, he replied truthfully, "Seldom."

"Why doesn't your answer surprise me?" she wondered aloud, grinning at him. Her fingers brushed the dark hair of his chest. She wished his unwavering confidence could rub off on her.

The smoldering look in his eyes told her he wanted to sweep her off her feet and carry her into his bedroom. All too easily, she could find it in her heart to forgive him. Even though he hadn't bothered to apologize.

She pulled her hands away from him. One step backward and he no longer touched her. The mental havoc he created with each stroke of his thumb began to subside. Slowly her head began to clear.

Right or wrong, she needed to nurse her grudge.

"It doesn't surprise you because you're in business for yourself," he answered simply. He followed her through the sliding door. "You have to make snap decisions. And act on them. There's little time for regrets."

Molly laughed. "A man makes snap decisions. When a woman does it, she's considered impetuous."

He solemnly shook his head in disagreement.

"It's true."

"How so?"

"Take what happened this morning, for instance. You drove off in my truck and left me here, stranded."

"You were exhausted."

"And you weren't?"

"No."

"Oh? Making love exhausted me and exhilarated you?"

Brandon shrugged off the difference. He leaned against the balcony rail, one ankle crossed over the other, his arms locked on his chest to keep from folding her into them.

"You were sound asleep. I was rarin' to go. So I did."

"In my truck," she reminded him. Growing increasingly exasperated, she accused, "And you'd do it again?"

"Nope," he drawled softly, staring at her mouth.

Just when she thought she'd gotten her point across, he added, "I'd take my truck."

Molly threw her hands up in the air in futility. "And drive straight to my office...to tend to *my* business."

"Actually," he said as he moved his hand to the side of her neck to calm her, "I dropped by my office first."

She had to force herself not to lean into his hand. She realized she'd made a strategic mistake when she'd strolled out to the balcony. Electric lighting and air-conditioning were far less romantic than moonlight and the fragrance of honeysuckle in full bloom. The chorus of summer sounds was a soothing symphony, taking the edge off her determination to make Brandon own up to having ulterior motives behind his acts of kindness.

Skipping over his minor transgressions, she blurted, "You have all the information you need to put Winsome out of business, don't you?"

He barely paid attention to what she'd said. He wanted to kiss her. As his fingers lazily massaged her neck, he was patiently waiting for her to finish talking so he could.

"Don't you?" she demanded when he began to lean down.

"Or save it."

"Save it? We don't need saving."

"I do," he countered, lowering his face until his mouth was directly above hers. "You're driving me crazy."

He settled his mouth on top of hers with blatant ownership. Molly, his heart beat. His Molly. It was how he'd thought of her while he'd pored over those damned computer sheets.

"Wait," she breathed. "I'm not going to spend the night here."

"Why not?"

She felt hot, and yet she shivered. "I hate hypocrites."

"Me, too." Brandon hushed her with another hot, soul-searching, openmouthed kiss. He made it impossible for her to utter a word. Again and again his mouth slanted across hers as his hands slid down her spine, intimately rubbing her.

She twisted her face away from his avaricious mouth. One of her fingers buttoned his lips. "Not you, Brandon. Me. I'm the hypocrite."

"Dammit, Molly." He nipped her finger, then laved it with his tongue. "Can't we finish this discussion later? Much later?"

"No!" Frustrated and distraught, she peeled herself from his arms. Tears filled her eyes. She blinked to hold them back. "I can't stay with you. If you won't talk to me, I might as well leave."

"You aren't going anywhere." He cuffed her wrist between his thumb and forefinger. If she wanted to talk, dammit, they'd talk! He strode to the wooden swing that hung at the end of the balcony, with her in tow behind him. He steadied the swing until she was seated. "Okay, Molly. Talk. You have my undivided attention. What's this nonsense about you being a hypocrite?''

"It's how I felt when I opened my mouth to scold my father for giving you the password," she explained. She'd dashed the tears from her eyes with the back of her hand before he could see them, but she could taste the salty tears she hadn't shed. She cleared her throat. "You want to eliminate your competition. We're virtually handing over Winsome Plumbing without a fight."

"Your father has no business climbing on roofs. Next time he falls, he could break his neck."

"There won't be a next time."

"How are you going to stop him?"

"By continuing to supervise at the construction sites myself."

Brandon disliked that idea. Immensely. Face-to-face, the construction workers were polite to women. But Molly was on the receiving end of several lustful stares when her back was turned. Yesterday he'd wanted to throttle half his crew for laying their eyeballs on her backside. There was no predicting what sort of trouble would be stirred up if the men knew she'd be there on a daily basis.

"No comment?"

She straightened her back against the wooden slats and folded her hands on her lap. She was trying to appear composed. It was an impossible feat with him towering over her, glaring down his nose disdainfully, as though she were a huckleberry solder flowing down a piece of pipe.

He hunkered down in front of her. "None. Yet."

Justifying her tentative decision, she added, "As you've said, John is getting too old to be climbing around in the rafters. I'm young. Agile. And capable."

"So you are," he agreed quietly.

He made a mental note to have a long talk with John Winsome. He figured her father's injuries would prevent him from returning to work for at least another month. Brandon had planned on coordinating her crews with his own. Plainly, she would reject his helping hand.

"I owe it to my father."

Brandon's scowl deepened. Family devotion was unfathomable to him. His own parents had left him in his grandfather's care before he was potty trained. The bond forged between him and John Winsome was stronger than the one with his own father.

"I haven't always been here when he needed me," she finished.

"Where were you?" Before he gave her a chance to reply, he said, "I heard that on the first day of kindergarten, you dumped the food from your lunch box and filled it with tools. You worked after school, during school breaks and over summer vacations. On your eighteenth birthday, you celebrated by taking the journeyman's test."

When he stopped for a breath, she interjected, "Who have you been talking to?"

"Anybody and everybody. Where you're concerned, I have an insatiable curiosity."

"The Winsome Whitewash," she scoffed. "Do you know where I was when Dad had his heart attack?"

"No. Where?"

"I couldn't be reached because I was on a Caribbean cruise." She twisted her hands together. Once she started the recriminations, she didn't seem able to stop. She wanted him to see that she wasn't the paragon of virtue he'd been led to believe. "Do you know where I was when he sold his Lincoln, hocked his guns and pawned my mother's wedding ring? Or what I was doing when he had to borrow money to make payroll?"

"Being a wife?" he guessed.

"Very astute," she replied starkly. Her chin sank an inch lower. "I failed there, too. The point is, Dad has always been there when I needed him. This is my one chance to prove myself worthy of the family name."

"Listen to me, Molly." He lifted her chin until their eyes met. "A man in the trades doesn't expect a woman to run his shop."

Her head snapped up higher. "Why not? Because women are weak and frail? Take another good look, Corral. This time without the rose-colored glasses."

"You have great legs." He risked infuriating her by trailing his hand down the calf of her leg. Better for her to be angry than morose. "Shapely. Long. Perfect."

She narrowed her eyes. "Are you telling me I'm too stupid to take over the business?"

"Whoa! You're jumping to the wrong conclusions again."

"Okay. Explain yourself. Why are you capable of running the exact same business? Single-handedly. One, I might point out, that is expanding by leaps and bounds."

"Testosterone?" he joked.

That lit her wick. She jumped off the swing as though jet-propelled.

"Where are you going?" He followed her doggedly as she stomped through his living area and down the steps. "Wait a minute, Molly. Don't go off half-cocked."

Over her shoulder, she gave him a dirty look. "You can thank your lucky stars I don't have a gun to go off half-cocked. Otherwise that big nose you've got stuck in my business would be pushing up petunias."

"C'mon, Molly." He grabbed; she dodged. "Stay here with me."

She darted to her truck, pulling her keys from her pocket as she ran. She was inside the cab, with the door locked, before Corral made it across the drive.

"I have to get back to town before the pharmacy closes. Male hormone pills don't require a prescription, do they?"

It was a great exit line!

Absolutely fabulous!

Amazingly succinct.

With a flick of the wrist, she saw her moment of verbal triumph fade.

"Don't be cantankerous," she urged Betsy. She pushed the clutch until she felt the floorboard and tried again. Nothing! "Dammit, at least sputter! Backfire! Start!"

Through the bug-splattered windshield, she watched a wide grin spread across Corral's face. Lackadaisically, he put his big, fat foot on Betsy's chrome bumper.

"Don't let him step on you." She released the emergency brake. Slowly the truck rolled backward.

His foot dropped to the concrete. Before she popped the clutch, she warned fiercely, "This is your last chance. You're a female, too. Don't you dare double-cross me!"

Betsy jerked, shuddered, then gave a loud buck-snort. Black smoke blew from the tail pipe. "Thata girl, Betsy. Give 'em a blast of estrogen out of your tail pipe!"

Chapter Nine

There were three days left until the end of the September billing period. She had to get those six red stickers removed.

Molly stroked the down arrow on the computer's keyboard. Images of the invoices Yolanda had prepared for the general contractors appeared on the blue screen. Mentally rounding off the numbers, subtracting the total from the amounts billed, she realized she'd be forced to take one of Corral's suppliers up on his credit offer unless she straightened out the red-sticker problem.

The thought of borrowing against future receivables made her stomach churn.

Exiting from one file into the next, she projected for the next thirty days. In three of the five subdivisions, several lots were scheduled to be scraped. Once the foundation boards were set and the sand moved in, the contractor would be ready for the crews to dig the trenches and lay pipe. That's where they made the highest profit. She juggled the figures in her head. Money from the grounds would pay the next month's supply bills for fixtures—tubs, toilets and shower bases.

With good weather and their work passing inspections, she'd be in good shape ... next month. Maybe. She tapped several keys to get back to the main menu.

All she had to do was make it through this month.

Funny, but she seemed to remember thinking the same thought *last* month!

Only, in August she was crunching the numbers to bid future work, while her father supervised the current jobs. She sorely missed John. Between the two of them she'd felt invincible, as though they could plumb the entire state of Texas. Now, with him out of action, she glanced at the stack of unfinished bid proposals on the corner of her desk and sighed. Somehow, in the next few days she had to get those bids completed. She raised her head to look at the map on the wall. Otherwise there would be fewer flags and they'd be faced with a very bleak winter.

"One day at a time," Yolanda advised from where she stood in the doorway. "Do I need to revise the invoices?"

Molly pushed back her chair from the desk. "No. I'll have those houses reinspected by Friday."

"Don't you think it's odd we're having inspection problems?" Yolanda crossed to the coffee urn. As she filled her cup, she said, "After all, the same men are doing the same work."

"Yeah, but the boss's shadow looming over their shoulders isn't the same." Molly raised her arms and stretched the kinks from her neck. "John spots trouble before it occurs."

"You may not be a great troubleshooter, but you brew a great cup of coffee. Much better than mine," Yolanda commended, inhaling the aroma before taking a sip. "What time did you get here?"

"I came back last night, did some catch-up work and slept on the couch."

"No wonder the pot is half-empty." Yolanda blew the steam and took another delicate sip before she brought up another touchy subject. "Did you change the computer's password?"

"No." She watched her secretary's brow crease in disapproval. "Corral won't be here."

"What do I do if he does arrive?"

"Page me."

"Sometimes it takes an hour for you to finish what you're doing and get to a phone. What am I supposed to do with Mr. Corral in the meantime?"

Molly grinned. "Shoot him. Is that what you want to hear?"

"Well, I have to admit, I didn't expect your father to give him free rein of the place. Nor did I expect John to tell me to smile and be *nice*." She swallowed a scalding gulp of coffee and grimaced. "Just because I threatened to permanently scar Mr. Corral's hand with an imprint of my teeth doesn't mean I was being uncooperative."

"Of course it doesn't," Molly agreed, trying to keep a straight face.

"You know who Mr. Corral reminds me of?"

"Who?"

"My second husband."

"Duncan?"

"Duncan was husband three. I mean Floyd. You remember him, don't you?"

"Short? Brown hair? Belt buckle big enough to serve a Thanksgiving turkey on?"

"With a beer belly that rolled it down flat. Yeah, that was number two."

"Sorry, Yolanda, but I don't see any similarities between the two of them."

"Not looks. Behavior. Floyd and Mr. Corral are both bundles of energy. Always giving orders. Do this. Do that. Not finished yet? Well, hop, hop, hop to it!"

"I can't imagine you letting any man order you around."

"That's the main reason I divorced him. But it wasn't the only reason." Yolanda paused, seeming to wait for Molly to ask for the reason. "Do you know why I divorced him?"

Molly shook her head. She'd given up on keeping track of Yolanda's love life.

"He mated like a jackrabbit, that's why!"

Laughing, Molly covered her embarrassment by shuffling two stacks of papers together. Brandon and Floyd certainly didn't have that in common. She didn't want to be reminded of how Brandon Corral made love. But a mental flash of his hands ever so slowly moving across her skin caused goose bumps down the side of her neck.

"I will say this," Yolanda added, rolling her dark eyes to the ceiling. "Mr. Corral is one handsome dude. But so was my first husband. Did I ever tell you about Roberto?''

Molly filed the papers in her bottom desk drawer. "What husband are you on now?"

"Number five."

"Didn't you tell me that you were marrying him because he made you forget the other men in your life?" Molly teased.

"In bed, I forget." She shook her hand as though her fingernails were on fire. "Believe me, your father wouldn't have had to tell me to be nice to Mr. Corral if it wasn't for my hubby. Joseph sets my tail feathers on fire. What about you?"

Choosing to misunderstand, Molly quipped, "I haven't met your latest."

"Not Joseph! Mr. Corral."

Molly removed her keys from her pocket. Sauntering to the door, she said, "I'll drop by to see Dad during lunch. Don't count me getting back here this afternoon. After I fix the problems at each house, I'll call you. You phone a reinspection in to the plumbing department. Okay?"

She was nearly to the door, when Yolanda's hearty chuckle stopped her.

"What's so funny?"

"You."

"What did I do?"

"Nothing. It's something I saw Mr. Corral do yesterday."

"What?"

Yolanda plucked the gold-framed picture off Molly's desk. "He was sitting there. Thinking real hard while he stared at the photograph of you and John."

"That's amusing?"

"He put his finger to his lips, then to the picture."
She grinned. "Since you're so closemouthed, I was
just wondering who Mr. Corral was kissing. You or
your dad?"

Molly bent over the hospital-bed railing and kissed
her father on the forehead. "You're looking better,
Dad. Much better."

"You look like you slept at the office," Kate Winsome groused, none too pleased with her daughter's
unkempt appearance.

"Stop fussing at her, Kate," John admonished.
"Molly doesn't have to rush home and throw something in the microwave for her husband the way you
do."

"Very funny, John. Keep it up and I'll ask the
hospital to cater your meals."

Molly filched a half-eaten sandwich from her
father's tray. Taking a small bite, she winked at him
and said, "Don't bother. Same chef."

She noticed John didn't hold his ribs or wince when
he laughed. Taking that as a good sign, she asked,
"When are they paroling you for good behavior?"

"Tomorrow."

"Great!" The meat tasted like charred cowhide,
but Molly ate it. "Morning or afternoon?"

"I want to get out before ten o'clock. That's when
the hospital bills for another day." John shifted restlessly. "It's bad enough—"

"We'll manage," Molly interjected, before her
parents started worrying about their lack of insur-
ance coverage.

She looked at her mother, who looked at John, who completed the circle by glancing up at his daughter.

"Next month will be better," the three of them chorused, laughing at the family joke.

"It will be," Molly promised. "Lots of grounds."

"We'll need them to pay for the supplies the whiz kid had delivered to the warehouse."

Molly pointed to the flourishing scrawl on John's leg cast. "You must be feeling stronger. For a while there I worried Corral had put his brand on you."

"Beholden, that's how I feel," John grumbled.

Kate placed her hand on her husband's shoulder. "Don't start."

"Start what?" Molly asked, finishing off the potato chips on his plate.

"Your father has this lamebrain idea that he's a charity case."

"When you take something without giving something back, it's charity," John said staunchly. "I don't like being beholden to any man."

"Me, neither," Molly concurred.

Kate grinned. "Guess the only thing for us to do is give him our firstborn," she joked, getting even for the snide remarks about her cooking.

"I accept." Brandon strolled into the room, looking like the cat who'd eaten a flock of canaries.

"I think you'd better ask John Junior first," Molly suggested, flashing her parents a broad wink.

She had the satisfaction of stopping Brandon in his tracks, even though it was temporary. From the hard glint in his eyes, she should have known he planned

on coming out on top in their game of one-
upmanship.

He moved next to her and brushed a kiss on her
lips.

"You're their one and only," he whispered.

Molly wasn't certain, but she thought she heard
"Mine, too."

"Excuse me?" Kate said, cupping her hand to her
ear. "Is there something going on that we should
know about?"

Flustered, Molly elbowed Corral in the ribs and
laughed. "He's only joking, Mother."

John picked up his book from the nightstand. "A
marriage of convenience? Lone Wolf married the
post commander's daughter to keep the peace.
Maybe—"

"The next time you give him a book," Molly interjected, "do us both a favor and make it the latest
edition of the plumbing code, would you?" The
blissful smile on her mother's face clued Molly that
within a heartbeat Kate would be ordering wedding
invitations and asking Corral for the names and addresses of his relatives. "The plumbing in wigwams
is substandard."

An orderly arriving gave Molly the opportunity she
needed to make a gracious exit, but she stood rooted
to the spot. No way was she going to leave the room
with the idea of a marriage-merger lingering in her
mother's mind.

"Good for you, Mr. Winsome," the orderly en-
thused. "You cleaned your plate."

She felt Brandon's hand at her elbow and stepped back to make room for the nurse, who'd followed the orderly into the room.

Quietly Brandon said, "I fixed the problem at the house on Spring Branch. Some kid must have dropped a rubber ball down the toilet. I had Yolanda call it in for inspection."

Earlier, Molly had augured a tennis ball out of a toilet in another house that had failed the final inspection. She frowned and bit her lower lip. An accident? It seemed highly unlikely the same type of obstruction would block two toilets in two different subdivisions.

Coincidence? Or malicious mischief?

She slanted a surreptitious glance up at the man who stood next to her. No, that's beneath Corral, she decided instantly. She'd have to see a video and the governor of Texas would have to notarize its authenticity before she'd believe Brandon capable of such a dirty trick.

"Stop worrying your lower lip, Molly," he chided. "I'm not Lone Wolf."

Glad he had misread her thoughts, she forced a smile on her lips and said, "Nobody could make you do anything you didn't want to do. You'd rather fight."

He nodded in agreement, but whispered close to her ear, "You might be able to convince me to wave the white flag."

"Surrender? You?"

"In a weak moment . . ."

"What are you two whispering about?" Kate asked inquisitively.

"Business," Molly replied. A scant second later Brandon answered, "John."

"John's business," Molly amended, quickly joining their two fibs into one whopping lie.

"Don't talk about me or my business as though I'm unconscious," John blustered. His face blanched to a ghostly gray. "What's going on?"

Molly shot Corral a speaking glance. "Business as usual."

"If I'd wanted you to lie to me I'd have sent you to law school. Now, let's hear the truth, Daughter. Be it good, bad or indifferent, I can take it."

"The inspectors are hassling her," Brandon volunteered, stepping between the bed and Molly.

"Hand me the phone," John instructed Brandon. "I can take care of that."

Molly skirted around Corral. "No need, Dad. I spoke to Mr. Hanson yesterday."

"And?"

"He sends his best wishes to you for a speedy recovery. Everything is under control." Silently she dared Corral to refute her statement.

John visibly relaxed. "That old codger has been around this business longer than I have. He thinks women belong in the kitchen, behind a hot stove."

"Oh no, John Winsome, you aren't going to start teasing me about my cooking." Kate covered his mouth with her hand. "It's time for your nap. When I remove my hand, smile and say, 'Goodbye, kids.'"

"Goodbye, kids." The look he gave his wife was filled with love. "Can't let her get too riled or she'll dip my boxer shorts in catnip and buy a mountain lion for a pet."

Laughing because John had spoken the honest-to-God truth, Kate walked Molly and Brandon to the door.

"Do you want me to make arrangements to get Dad home tomorrow?" Molly asked her mother.

"If you mean you'll clean out the tools from the back of the truck and put a lounge chair in it . . . no."

"Dad's idea?" Molly replied, shaking her head in disbelief.

Kate nodded. "Knowing your father, he'd probably have you drive him around to each job on the way home."

"Don't worry, Mother. I'll borrow Yolanda's car."

"That isn't necessary," Brandon stated in a voice that brooked no refusal. "I'll drive John and Kate home."

Kate hugged Brandon. "You're a fine young man, Brandon Corral. You must do your mama proud."

The down-home compliment and bear hug punched a soft spot in his heart. This hug was far different from the embrace he was accustomed to receiving from his own mother. Although the hospital corridor was as busy as the airport terminal, Kate wasn't the least bit inhibited about showing her affection for him. His eyes felt misty. Mortified by how such a small gesture could reduce a grown man to tears, he gave Kate an awkward thump on the back and stepped aside and watched how Molly hugged her mother.

No loose-limbed hug. No air kisses. Molly locked her mother in her arms and planted a hearty kiss on her cheek. Despite their banter, it was obvious the two women loved and respected each other.

Just observing them partially filled the lonesome hole in his soul.

Admit it, Corral, you're tired of being on the outside—like a tail-wagging puppy in a pet store with his nose pressed up against the window. A yearning from deep within made him want to mean more to Molly Winsome than a wet nose print on a windowpane.

He wanted to be loved. He wanted to be part of the bear hugs and smacking kisses. Only then would he feel as though he had the family he'd been denied.

"What is he doing?" Molly muttered, feeling damned foolish for arriving after Corral had fixed her men's screwup. She heaved her toolbox into the bed of the truck. "Doesn't he have his own business to run?"

I promised your father I'd help take care of his business.

Corral was as good as his word. On numerous occasions, she'd failed to convince him that his help wasn't needed. She could manage. Temporarily, at least. Until John recovered.

With each fragmented thought, she lifted a piece of electrical equipment into her truck.

She checked her printout list. Three down, three to go. Her finger underlined the next address, then moved down. If Corral was headed down the same column of addresses, she'd get one jump ahead of him.

Two hours later, she twirled her pipe cutter around the three-inch main line of a two-story house. Burt, Cliff and Harold, her most reliable top-out crew, had completed this water pipe. There shouldn't be a problem, she mused.

When she'd tested the faucet in the master bath, initially water had gushed from the spout. Within seconds, the flow was down to a dribble. Trying the faucets in the other bathrooms, she had the same results. The problem had to be in the main line that fed water to each fixture.

Her diagnosis had her on a ladder, in the rafters, cutting pipe near the riser leading to the top floor.

"Something is plugging it," she mumbled, removing a six-foot length of copper.

She held the pipe to her eye. A row of lines appeared to cut the diameter of the pipe in two. Puzzled, she dropped the end of the pipe on the concrete floor to break loose whatever was stuck inside. Nothing fell out.

She looked around for something to shove down the hole. The floor had been swept. Frustrated, she swung the pipe against a stud, then banged it on the floor several times. With each stroke, she heard a scrape as the objects became dislodged.

As she poked her finger into the pipe, a handful of what appeared to be oversize plug nickels spilled into her hand. Perplexed, Molly dropped them in her front shirt pocket. She had a mental picture of the disks of metal flowing through the copper line, tilting up and blocking the water when the pressure increased, working like a flutter valve.

This was no accident.

Sabotage?

As Molly cleaned the ends of pipe with sand cloth, fluxed them and joined the two pieces with a cou-

pling, she tried to piece together several incidents that
had occurred during the past week. John's accident
had happened while he was attempting to install a
roof flashing. The wrong grade of pipe had been used
in a building. Balls mysteriously clogged toilets. And
now she'd found stray pieces of metal causing block-
ages in the main line.

She removed the striker from her belt and twisted
the valve on the B-tank. A spark jumped to the tip of
her torch when she squeezed the striker. Orange flame
jetted from the torch. She adjusted the regulator until she saw only an intense, hot, blue flame. She
heated the coupling, then swiped the tip of a roll of
solder at the edges. Silver solder sucked between the
pipe and fitting. She used her glove to wipe off the
excess solder.

Brandon watched. Perched on the top rung of her
ladder, absorbed in her work, Molly hadn't noticed
him. One look and he knew exactly what difficulty
she'd encountered and what she'd found: silver coins.

Inside his pocket, his hand rubbed two half-dollars
against each other. Unlike the ball that had floated to
the top of the pipe, the coins had moved with the flow
of water. He'd had a devil of a time finding them.

He hated being the bearer of bad news—especially
when he knew what logical conclusion Molly would
draw.

As she started down the ladder, Brandon stepped
forward and took the cumbersome tank for her.

"One more red sticker taken care of," Molly said,
lithely swinging her toolbox down to the concrete
floor. She reached into her shirt pocket. "Electrician
blanks."

Brandon tried to read the inscrutable expression on her face as he reached into his jeans pocket. Her blue eyes didn't flash, burning holes in him. Slowly he opened his palm. "Coins."

"Same difference. What kind of ball did you find stopping up the toilet at the first house you went to?"

"A tennis ball."

"I didn't want to think anything of it when you mentioned it at the hospital." Twin lines of distress marred her forehead. "But guess what I found when I pulled the toilet at the first house on the failed inspection list?"

"Another ball?"

Molly nodded. She reached for the coins in his hand; his fingers closed around hers. Her troubled eyes rose to meet his.

"I know what you're thinking, Molly."

"Do you?" Smiling wanly, she hummed a few bars of a Garth Brooks song. "Are you a mind reader or did you borrow my crystal ball?"

"Neither." Surprised she wasn't hurling accusations at him, he inverted his hand. Quarters and nickels fell into the palm of her hand. "Who do you think did this?"

Molly sighed. "I haven't the faintest idea."

Relieved she hadn't flung the coins in his face and accused him, he asked, "Have any of your crews reported problems with men in the other trades?"

"No." Minor squabbles between the plumbers, electricians and framers were common on constructions sites. "The blanks I removed are from electrical switch boxes, but..."

"But what?"

"Unless I'm mistaken, Rosenthal Electric did this job. Jebson Electric did the house where you were. If it's a feud, we're talking about two plumbing crews and two electrical crews. I can't fathom that."

"I can't, either. A carpenter would punch nail holes through the pipe or fill the pipe with glue."

"Only a plumber would know how much trouble a ball or a pocketful of coins can cause." Stymied, Molly uttered an impatient oath. "Who'd do this?"

"Somebody who'd benefit from damaging Winsome's good reputation. Or someone who knows you're short on capital." Brandon picked up her equipment. He gestured for her to precede him, and they left the building. He stowed her gear before he said, "A competitor."

"You?"

The disbelief he heard in her voice pleased him. "Yeah, *me*. Corral Plumbing."

"You'd be the last person on my list of suspects."

"Why?"

"Call it female intuition," she replied, trying to smile, but not having the heart. A few weeks ago, she would have resoundingly jumped to that conclusion. At that time she had considered Brandon her enemy, her adversary, the man who wanted to take over Winsome Plumbing by hook or by crook. If she still mistrusted him, she sure as hell wouldn't have shared his bed. The weight of Winsome Plumbing's normal everyday problems staggered her. Trouble of this nature was almost too much to bear. "Please, no confessions. I'd really and truly hate being wrong about your innocence."

The bleakness Brandon saw and heard tore at him. His throat constricted. Swallowing hard, he made a genuine effort to reassure her. "We'll find him."

"Who has time to play detective?" She wiped her brow on the back of her brown cotton glove and looked up at the sun. It had to be a hundred degrees in the shade. Heat and lack of sleep made her feel that the temperature was subzero. "Right now, my give-a-damner is broken."

When she moved toward Betsy's door, Brandon stopped her by saying softly, "For what it's worth, I think you're doing one helluva good job, Molly."

"Thanks." His praise lifted her spirits. "I have to take care of the last red sticker. It's an easy one—installing an air chamber. Would you fill these pipes with water, then meet me there?"

Pleased she wanted him to help her, he answered, "I'll be right behind you."

"One more favor, please? Would you use your cellular phone to call this one in to Yolanda? She'll phone the inspector's office." On second thought, Molly reached into her pocket and flipped him one of the coins he'd found in the pipe. "Use this. It'll make me feel better to know the vandal paid for the call."

"Poetic justice?" Brandon grinned.

"On a small scale. The time we wasted finding the problem cost a heck of a lot more than fifty cents."

As she drove to the next repair job, she mentally made a list of things to do that required more hours than were left in the day. After she installed the air chamber, she still had to check the list of materials the men needed and get the things ready for tomorrow morning. Plus go over the daily office paperwork.

Maybe by midnight she'd eke out a few minutes to work on those bids.

Counting her blessings, she silently thanked Brandon for ordering the materials. Otherwise she would have had to rush to the office, do a quick inventory and call the suppliers in time for them to make a late-afternoon delivery.

If he hadn't barged into her office, taking part of the overload on his broad shoulders, she'd be neck deep in trouble. She hated to admit it, but without Corral's help she would never have gotten those stickers removed in time to turn in the invoices to the general contractors. No paychecks on the tenth of the month...Lord have mercy, she didn't know what she would have done then. Her men deserted her if she couldn't meet the payroll.

Her grimace inverted as she had a pleasant thought. Lone Wolf Corral would have had to rescue her. And then he would have belonged to her. Wasn't that the code of the Old West? Whether it was or wasn't, Molly liked the idea of a woman owning a man, for a change. Let the men be the wives; it's what every woman needed.

Chapter Ten

Through the bathroom window, Molly saw Brandon lay a strip of tire rubber as he rounded the corner. His timing was perfect, she thought, turning off the gas valve. She felt good about getting the air chamber installed in an expeditious manner. With the worst part of her day behind her, she could actually smile over Corral's eagerness to be with her.

"Molly! Molly!"

"Upstairs, Brandon," she shouted. "I'll be down as soon as I gather up my tools."

She could hear him taking the steps two at a time. Eager? Her smile grew. She'd welcome a few minutes of "dallying"—that's what her mother called kissing; it would clear the gas fumes from her head.

Briskly she strode toward the sound of his footsteps. As he turned the blind corner, she let him bump into her. His hands reflexively grabbed her shoulders; his mouth opened, just in time for her to kiss him.

Her kiss was unexpected, but he was delighted, and put the urgent reason for rushing up the steps temporarily on hold. Bad news could wait.

His tongue danced with hers, circling and swirling, mating. He lifted her higher into his arms, until her arms circled his neck.

Oh, Molly, love, he thought, despairing over how to tell her. Given a choice, he wanted their passion to take them to a quiet place where there were no business problems and her father's health didn't matter. He wanted the fire of their passion to burn through the hazy fog of torment threatening to engulf both of them.

"Molly, sweetheart . . ."

"Don't talk, Corral." She backed him against the wall. Leaning heavily against him, she peppered kisses along his smoothly shaven jaw. "Good guys deserve a proper thank-you."

"Stop, sweetheart . . ." He gripped her shoulders, pushing her away from him. "You've got to go to the hospital. Your mother needs you."

With a tiny shake of her head, Molly said, "Mother needs me? Mother?"

"She collapsed when they wheeled your father out of the room." He pulled her against his chest. He wanted to absorb the shock and pain Molly felt. So far, he'd done a bad job of relaying what Yolanda had told him. There must be a kinder, gentler way, but damned if he knew what it was. "It's his heart."

"A heart attack?" Molly gasped.

"No, not yet. The doctors are trying to prevent one."

"And Mother? Is she okay?"

"She asked for you before she lost consciousness."

Molly's entire body shuddered as she rejected what she couldn't comprehend. First Dad. Now Mother? Both of them?

No! God, no!

She wouldn't believe it. Her parents were strong, healthy. This couldn't be happening to them, to her! She sagged against him as though she'd been hit between the shoulder blades with an ax.

"Let's go." Brandon wrapped his arm around her waist, supporting her, turning her to the steps. "No argument. You're too shaken up to drive by yourself."

Through tear-filled eyes, she let him take complete control and lead her to his truck. What would life be like without her parents? She heard Brandon's sympathetic words, but they seemed coded. Nothing registered other than the sharp agony of knowing she could lose both of them on the same day.

She needed Brandon's strength. Without him, she would never make it down the steps of the house and into his Suburban.

Brandon did his best to comfort her. Silently he cursed his ineptness. Perspiration beaded on her upper lip, and yet her skin felt clammy. His own hands trembled as he awkwardly pulled her across the bench seat.

"Are you okay?"

The blank look she gave him scared the hell out of him. Was she in shock? On television, people going into shock were brought out of it with a sharp slap. Brandon held her face against his shoulder. He couldn't bring himself to slap her, even for her own good.

"I want to be alone with her," Molly said, wiping the corners of her eyes. They were dry. Her throat felt raw from stoically swallowing her sobs.

Upon their arrival, the head nurse had apprised them of John's and Kate's current status. Neither of their lives was in imminent danger. But the what-ifs and what could have happened continued to frighten Molly.

Brandon nodded. "I'll be in the lounge. Waiting. I'll be here for as long as you need me."

For as long as you need me. For as long as you need me.

His promise echoed in her mind as she looked up at him. Hadn't her parents promised to be there for as long as she needed them? Some promises could not be kept, not forever, not her parents' nor Brandon's. No matter how honestly given, they'd be broken eventually.

"No. Don't wait." Don't make promises you can't keep. "I'll page you if either of them changes for the worse."

Brandon enfolded her in his arms. "You're sure you don't want me to stay?"

"You have things to do."

"They can wait."

Emotionally vulnerable, she allowed herself the luxury of clinging to him. Her fingers dimpled the back of his shirt she held him so tightly. She could stand on her own. She could. But for a few short moments she wanted to pretend that she didn't have to be alone.

"I'll talk to you later," she said, forcing her arms to drop to her sides.

Molly gave him a brave smile as she squared her shoulders, but the soles of her shoes dragged against the polished tiles when she entered the hospital room.

She expected Kate to be sedated. Her mother was sitting up, wide-awake, with fire in her eyes.

"What did I tell you?" Kate demanded, as she scrambled the cards she'd been playing. "You laughed at me when I told you about Maude. Well, I'm here to tell you—they aren't taking my right breast!"

For a second, Molly stood at the foot of the bed, completely confused. Maude? Maude who? Then she remembered. The star of Kate's favorite television soap opera. The night John had been admitted into the hospital, her mother had vowed not to take any naps because of what had happened on that program.

Molly opened her mouth to ask how her mother was feeling, then snapped it shut when Kate spoke. "Your father started having chest pain. I must have fainted. The next thing I knew, the nurses had me flat on my back and were poking and prodding, sticking me with needles." Kate looked peeved. "How's John? Nobody'll tell me anything."

"I talked to the head nurse. Dad's blood pressure has stabilized. They're monitoring him closely as a precautionary measure." To calm her mother, Molly moved to the chair closer to the bed, sat down and asked softly, "Aren't you supposed to be resting?"

"I'm fine," Kate snapped.

"Sure you are."

"Don't you *mother* me in that tone of voice, young lady. I'm telling you, I won't shut my eyes until your father is back in this room. I need him. He needs me." With that pronouncement, Kate jiggled the bed rail. "Get me out of here."

The rail collapsed. Kate swung her legs off the bed before Molly could stop her. Any doubts Molly had about her mother's state of health were appeased when Kate rose on her bare feet, tightened the knot on her belt and declared imperiously, "I'm going to the bathroom. Alone."

Molly picked up the deck of cards from the bed tray. As a child, she and her mother had whiled away many hours playing gin rummy while they waited for John. She dealt two hands. In this abnormal situation, doing something normal would be good for both of them.

Several minutes later, Kate rejoined her. She noticed Kate had freshened her makeup. Also, she'd changed into a pair of navy blue slacks with a matching top. From the defiant tilt of her chin, it was apparent that nobody was going to get her back into bed.

"Want to play rummy?" Molly suggested.

"Do I have to let you win?"

Molly grinned at the rhetorical question. In Kate's book, being a good mother did not include building false self-esteem. Her mother played to win. It took skill and a healthy dose of good luck to beat her. And heaven help her if she dared to cheat.

"I dealt." Molly fanned her cards. "You discard."

"I'll knock for ten," Kate said, laying down two spreads and several cards that totaled ten points in value.

Molly tossed down her cards. "Luck."

"Count 'em and weep," Kate gloated.

During the next two hours, Molly wept. "If we were playing for money, you'd own Winsome Plumbing."

"Your father lost the company to me before you were born," Kate quipped, shuffling the cards. "How are you and Brandon Corral getting along?"

Wondering what had caused the jump from one subject to the next, Molly carefully considered her reply. "We won't lose the company to him, if that's worrying you."

Kate laughed. "I'm not worried. I have faith in you."

"Corral has been a big help," she confessed, feeling as though she'd be cheating to take full credit.

"You like him, don't you?"

"Deal," Molly said, reluctant to confide in her mother.

"Scared?"

"Of what?"

"Falling for the wrong guy." Kate began to deal, slowly. "Again. Once bitten, twice shy?"

"Corral isn't anything like Leon."

"They are both handsome," Kate replied, comparing the two men. "Both from well-to-do families. Both successful businessmen. Both attracted to you."

"Faster, Mother. Deal faster. I feel a no-brainer coming on." She wanted a no-brainer, a hand she didn't have to concentrate on, while she dodged her mother's inquisition.

Kate glanced at the score pad. "Ten points and I'm out. Do you think divorced women make the same mistakes twice?"

"I think . . ." Molly sorted her hand and scowled. At first glance, it appeared that she had one of each kind in all four suits. No sets. No runs. "You must be stacking the deck."

"Do you think Brandon is looking for a wife?"

"I think . . . you need this card." Molly discarded the queen of hearts.

Kate picked it up and used her elbow to shove the card in place. "Gut-card. Thanks."

Groaning, Molly drew from the deck. She'd achieved the impossible—a card that didn't match anything she held in her hand. To get rid of a card that would count the most against her, she took a chance and discarded the queen of clubs. "Take that."

Kate did.

"You said the queen of hearts was a gut-card," Molly accused.

"It was." Kate proved it by putting her cards face-up on the tray. "Gin."

Not bothering to count her points, she drew two lines under Kate's side of the sheet. "Losers cry deal."

"That's your problem, Molly."

Molly picked up the cards and shuffled. "You're right. New game. I get to deal."

"No, I meant you holding out for gin. You want it all or nothing. You can't win that way. Sometimes you have to take a chance and knock . . . early."

"Ten for me. Eleven for you," Molly counted. Is this a lesson in gin rummy or my love life? she wondered. Her mother's poker face held no answers. Without looking at her cards, she flipped them face-up. "Knock."

Surprised by her daughter's audacity, Kate matched two sets and one run. Molly had a small card left over. With a grimace, she counted the points in her hand. "You got me."

"Well, I'll be damned," Molly said, amazed by her luck.

"No, you'll be blessed," Kate contradicted. "You've done your duty by calming me down. Why don't you go do something for yourself? Like catching up with Brandon Corral and asking him the questions I asked you?"

Molly grinned. "And get off this winning streak? Uh-uh. Count them up, Mother."

An hour later, in the midst of Molly soundly waxing Kate, the nurse came in and informed them John would be returning shortly.

After the nurse left the room, Kate's hands trembled as she covered her face and said a prayer of gratitude. Molly seconded it. Not only for her fa-

ther's reprieve, but for her mother's inner strength.
She realized that while her mother had been deeply
concerned for John, she'd distracted Molly from her
fears.

"Mercy, I almost forgot." Kate handed Molly the
book Brandon had loaned John. "John jotted down
some notes for you on the back page. Business, I
suppose. I didn't read it."

From her office, Molly paged Brandon. She'd
stayed at the hospital until John had been returned to
his hospital bed and fallen asleep. Now she was following her mother's sage advice: take a chance and
knock early.

She settled back in her desk chair and waited. It
was dark when she left the hospital, too dark to read
her father's instructions. How like him, she thought
fondly, to use anything handy to write on. She opened
the book to the last page.

"Coppertop," she read aloud, smiling as she continued to read silently:

Call this an old man's foolishness or a premoni-
tion of what's to come. I woke up this morning
feeling I'd left too much unsaid.

Have I told you I'm proud of you? I am. And
how much I love you? I do.

Whatever happens to me, even if it seems final, don't you and your mother grieve. I want
both of you to think of me as having gone to the
shop early. You may not see me, but I'll be there
watching over you. The three of us won't be
separated forever. Love and devotion never die.

When it's your turn to cross over, I'll be there, waiting for you.

Always.
John

The phone rang as she finished reading her father's name. Choked up, tears cascading down her face, she picked up the receiver.

"Hello?" Her voice cracked.

"Molly?"

"Yes." She pulled a tissue from her middle drawer. As she wiped her nose, sniffling, a small sob came from the back of her throat.

"Are you crying?"

"Not exactly." His concern decimated her composure. Between hiccuped sobs, she begged, "Can you come over here? Please?"

"I'm on my way."

Brandon hung up without saying goodbye. She knew she could count on him. Since the accident, he'd saved her sanity at least half-a-dozen times, but who was counting?

She blew her nose hard, then yawned until her ears popped. It was a trick her mother had taught her. Mopping her face with another tissue, she realized kindness cost her more tears than heartache. She didn't cry when she was hurt; she cried when someone touched her heart.

Molly barely had time to wash her face and run a comb through her hair before she heard the front door rattle.

"Molly, it's me. Let me in!" Brandon roared.

He'd made a thirty-minute drive in less than twenty. Half the Austin Police Department should be chasing him. One thought had held the gas pedal to the floorboard: Molly needed him.

With the peculiar incidents that had happened recently, his imagination had gone wild. A locked door wasn't going to constrain him. He took several steps backward, bent his arm so his elbow would act as a battering ram and charged forward—just as the door opened wide.

Quick reflexes alone prevented him from driving his elbow into Molly's chest. At the last second, his arms stiffened perpendicular to his body. His palms slammed against the metal siding of the building. A harsh jolt of impact traveled from his hands to his shoulders.

"Damn!" he shouted, feeling as though his wrists, elbows and shoulders were cymbals being crashed together. *"Son of a bitch!"*

"What are you doing?" Molly gasped. She braced her shoulder under his arm and helped him into the reception area. "That was the damnedest thing I've ever seen anybody do."

"I don't doubt it," he said between clenched teeth. He collapsed into a leather chair before his knees gave out beneath him. "Hurt like hell, too."

Swiftly Molly ran her fingers along the length of his arms. It was a miracle he hadn't broken a bone—several bones.

"You could have waited until I opened the door."

"Fear and impetuosity are a dangerous mix," he said dryly. The movement of her hands exacerbated the pain. He pulled her down on his lap. "I called.

You were crying, talking in a hushed voice. I thought you were in physical danger. I *literally* jumped to the wrong conclusion."

"The door was locked, so you decided to break it down?"

"Don't give me any sass about being able to take care of yourself."

Molly wrapped her arms around his neck, holding him close while she anointed the crown of his head with several kisses. "You're something else, Brandon Corral."

He raised his face to look at her. Her blue eyes spoke volumes, but that wasn't enough. He needed to hear the words. "Am I?"

"Yeah." She brushed her mouth against his. "You're special. Very special."

Brandon sighed with contentment. "Next time I'll use my head," he promised.

"As a ram? Please! Don't."

Chuckling, he rephrased what he'd meant. "I'll think before I leap."

"Good. I wouldn't want to be responsible for you hurting yourself."

Brandon shut his eyes. "Then quit squirming on my lap."

Aware she was no featherweight, she started to get up. "Why don't we go back in my office?"

"Not until you tell me why you were crying."

"I'll show you," she promised, lithely scooting off his lap. "It's a letter."

"A threatening letter?"

Molly grinned, took his hand and pulled him from the chair. "No. Dad wrote it. I can't explain why it made me cry. You'll have to read it to understand."

Inside her office, she gestured for him to be seated on the sofa. He kicked off his shoes and stretched out full-length on the sofa. She gave him the historical novel and curled up beside him.

"Dad jots down notes on anything handy. It's on the last page."

She watched Brandon read the personal note. When he closed the book, his fingers followed the embossed lettering on the front cover, then he turned to her and said, "Thank you for sharing that with me."

"John has heart trouble," she explained, holding the book close to her chest.

"He must have recognized the symptoms and written this to you." Molly nodded. After she'd set the book aside, he cuddled her against him. "Everlasting love that crosses the boundaries of eternity," he murmured, gazing into her eyes. "You inspire it."

"Do I?"

"Passion. Devotion. Loyalty," he said between the small kisses he spread across her cheeks. His rough hands pushed beneath her shirttail, massaging the tense muscles of her back.

His praise pleased her, but the good Lord knew she'd made more than her share of mistakes. Any woman who'd suffered the agonies of heartbreak learned to be cautious, very cautious. She no longer trusted her instincts to tell the difference between truth and lies, honesty and dishonesty.

But surely falling in love with Brandon Corral wouldn't be another mistake, would it? He'd never want to change her, to make her into something she could never be, would he?

Molly arched against him, sinking her hands in his hair and closing her eyes. She didn't want to worry about yesterdays or tomorrows or eternity. Better to concentrate on the delicious sensations of his hands and mouth on her skin.

Lowering his head, Brandon dragged his lips across her throat. "Talk to me," he urged. "Tell me what you're thinking."

"Now?"

He raised his head, trying to read her expression. "We're about to be as intimate as a man and woman can be." He tapped her temple with one finger. "Do you know the difference between making love and sex?"

She grinned. "This isn't a joke, is it?"

"Hell, no."

"Then you tell me the difference. Don't make me wait for a punch line."

"Ninety percent of making love takes place up here." He smoothed the faint wrinkles on her brow. "Ninety percent of sex takes place below the belt."

She nodded, drawing her own conclusion. "I think..."

"No polite lies," he warned. He needed to be inside her, in her thoughts, where it counted. "Not even ones you think are for my own good."

"We make love," she finished saying, loudly, as though the volume would quiet her doubts and fears.

"But you're not certain?"

Her voice was barely audible when she answered truthfully, "I'm afraid to love."

Brandon felt that he was finally getting somewhere with her. Rolling her on top of him, he asked solemnly, "Why?"

"It's not you," she reassured him, not wanting to hurt his feelings. "It's me. It's taken five years of diligent research to find the real me, the real Molly Winsome. I don't want to lose my identity again."

"Is that what love does?"

"To me it did. I changed."

"How?"

"In every way. How I looked, dressed, talked, walked . . . and thought. I hated the *new* me. She was useless, a phony. I hated myself. It was no surprise to me when the divorce papers arrived. How could I expect my husband to love me when I didn't like who I was?" With a deep sigh, she said, "I don't need another Henry Higgins in my life."

For a second, he couldn't recall anyone by that name, then he remembered the old movie *My Fair Lady.* Henry Higgins had changed a flower girl with a cockney accent into a lady and presented her to a fake, mysterious prince.

Smiling down at her, he said, "I like your Southern drawl and the way you dress."

Molly pushed against his shoulder, rolling him over on his back, and pinned him down by sprawling across his chest. "What about you, Brandon? Why haven't you fallen in love? Why aren't you married with two or three kids?"

"I have a demanding mistress . . . Corral Plumbing."

"That's an excuse. We both know you have plenty of time." Verbally tweaking his nose, she added, "Admit it. You're a confirmed bachelor. You'll never get married."

"I made time for you."

"No. You made time for Winsome Plumbing."

He tugged on the braid that had fallen across her shoulder. "You don't really believe that, do you?"

"What should I believe?" Before he could unbind her braid, she reclaimed it. To appeal to his strong sense of fairness, she said, "I told you the truth. Why can't you do the same?"

Brandon turned his head away from her. His eyes grew troubled as he glanced around her office. He searched his mind for another glib reply. His gaze focused on the book with the message John had written to her.

She forked his chin between her hand. "Uh-uh. You're the one who wanted to share the unvarnished truth. Don't pretty it up for me."

Slowly Brandon shook his head, disengaging her fingers from his face. How could she understand? Her family was close-knit. John and Kate hadn't rejected her at birth.

"Tell me," Molly insisted relentlessly.

He knew she wasn't going to let him off easily. He felt cornered, and yet strangely enough he wanted to confide in her. He sensed a feeling of warmth and acceptance radiating from her that melted his stoic reserve.

"I have," he began. "Partially. Remember the other day at Barton Springs when I told you I didn't want to produce any unwanted children?"

"Yeah?"

Brandon took a deep breath to steady his nerves before he admitted, "I am one."

"What in the world makes you think your parents don't love you?"

He'd pulled her head against the crook of his shoulder and neck so her eyes couldn't see his expression, but he heard the note of disbelief in her voice. "My parents unofficially abandoned me before I was out of diapers."

"*Un*officially?"

"I wasn't put up for adoption." He tried to make light of his despair. "While they gallivanted around the world, they sent tokens of their love. My room at my grandfather's house looked like an airport gift shop. Stuffed animals of every size and shape. Exotic jars of food. A shrunken head from the Amazon River Valley."

"Ugh."

Brandon grinned. "I just said that to see if you'd fallen asleep."

"I'm awake and listening."

"And T-shirts from everywhere," he continued. "Postcards with 'Having fun, wish you were here' scribbled on them. Funny, but they forgot 'love' before they signed their names."

"Not funny," Molly said, silently substituting *sad, tremendously sad*. "Child neglect is never humorous."

"I wasn't neglected, Molly. I lived in a mansion overlooking Town Lake, with ten servants at my beck and call. My grandfather provided me with—"

"Love?" she interjected.

"In his fashion," Brandon agreed. "Between you and me, he got more excited about a new model of Lincoln coming off the production line than by anything I did. This is an exaggeration, but I used to tell my fraternity brothers that I was a junior in college before my grandfather realized I'd moved out of his house. He wouldn't have noticed then if I hadn't driven off in one of his classic Lincolns."

Brandon forced a chuckle between his lips. "This sounds worse than it was. A kid with money has to be ugly as sin or stingy not to be popular. I was never alone. Loneliness comes from within, Molly. There's a difference."

"It's a state of mind? Like making love?"

"Or thirst. When I'm with you I feel as though I'm neck deep in pure, sparkling water. Sometimes I'm afraid I'll sink before I can drink my fill. At other times I'm afraid you're a mirage and I'll die of thirst."

Molly braced her arms next to his shoulders, slowly raising her torso. "Make love to me, Brandon. Let me love you."

Her fingers threaded through his dark hair as his mouth closed over hers. She deepened the kiss. She couldn't taste the bitterness of his years of neglect, only the sweetness of his rising ardor.

With the greatest care, he removed her clothing, then his own. What could have been awkward was beautiful because his dark eyes caressed her skin with reverence. His lips and hands, a contrast in moistness and dryness, stroked each feminine mound and curve he disrobed. He made no false promises or vows of undying love, and yet he showed her he cared with each loving touch, each kiss.

As she sat perched astride him, her heart slammed against her ribs so violently she felt dizzy. Reflexively she caught his forearms to maintain her balance, digging her nails into his hard flesh. Her mind clouded with heat as he explored her breasts with his fiery mouth, sipping gently, then suckling her until small whimpering noises expressed how much she wanted him.

A spray of goose bumps spread around him and led him into her welcoming femininity. For long moments he held both of them perfectly still, as though he could suspend them in time and motion. Deep within her, he wanted to brand her as his, so no other man would ever think of trespassing.

She circled her hips, beckoning him to climb quickly to the heights of rapture, but he held back. With the tip of his tongue he removed the tiny beads of dampness above her lips, attempting to tame the wildness inside her. His own body gleamed with sweat, and his dark hair was wet.

The urgent expression on her face and the tight hold of her fingers on the flesh of his hips signaled him not to prolong the sweet agony too long. With the heel of his hand nestled against the damp curls between her thighs, he parried each thrust of her hips. His entire being focused on her, reading each response she gave him.

A tingling sensation traveled from her heels up to the calves of both legs, then journeyed to the nerve endings in her scalp. Her knees gripped his hips; her buttocks clenched. Her blue eyes glazed over with pleasure as the glorious sensations rippled through-out her body.

Their lovemaking was wild and intense, yet tender and gentle. There was only Brandon, a loner needing to be loved, and Molly, a nurturer needing to give love. Just as their minds had come together, so did their bodies. Two halves became one and the whole was stronger, more resilient, closer to the perfection they both sought.

...

...

...

Chapter Eleven

"Hey, boss lady," Brandon murmured against Molly's tangled hair. "Rise and shine. It's gonna be a beautiful day in sunny Texas."

"Ummmm," Molly moaned, blinking as she awakened. Late, late last night, she'd fallen asleep sprawled on top of Brandon. "You make one fine mattress, Corral. Lumpy in all the right places. Don't move. Push the snooze alarm, would you?"

Reluctant to start the day himself, he tickled her nose with the blunt tip of a lock of her hair. A blanket of silk, he thought, loving the way she scrunched up her nose. One of us has to be practical. He grinned. Molly would blush for weeks if Yolanda arrived and found them naked, entwined in a lovers' embrace on the couch.

"I have to get the supplies ready for your men before I go to my warehouse," he said, putting his priorities in the order of what he had to do. "One of us has to make coffee."

"I will." Fair was fair. He'd left a pot brewing for her the first night they'd spent together. She slid to his side to let him get up. "You're welcome to use the shower."

Her sleepy eyes widened as she watched him stand, then cross the room. She smiled. "Cute butt, Corral."

"Glad you noticed," he answered, casting a cocky grin at her to cover his embarrassment while he pulled on his jeans.

"Actually, it's one of the first things I noticed about you. Remember? You were coming down the ladder, with the beam from my flashlight—"

"Molly, stop!"

"Why?"

"Because my zipper is going to sever your love life if you keep talking."

Giggling, she picked her shirt up off the floor and pulled it over her head. She stood, pulling it down to midthigh. She was reaching under her collar to pull her hair from beneath her shirt, when she noticed Brandon watching her.

"Touché," he gloated when her face turned pink. "I wouldn't mind sharing the shower and skipping the coffee."

"That's big of you."

"Not yet," he countered, "but it could be."

He'd lost her, but she caught up with his train of thought when he glanced meaningfully at the front of his jeans.

"You're wicked, Corral," she replied with a sassy grin. "Go take your shower. Alone."

"Okay." He obliged without argument. "Would you mind getting the change of clothes out of my truck for me?"

"Fetch and carry? You aren't trying to turn me into your body servant, are you?" she teased, winking at him.

"Body servant? Naw," he drawled, exaggerating his swagger as he strode toward the bathroom. "But I'd like a love slave, one who caters to my every lascivious whim. Care to apply for that position?"

"Can't."

"Why not?"

She grinned, nodding toward the couch. "Because the position was filled. Last night."

"So it was," he agreed with a smug smile. "So it was."

"I'll get your clothes, if you get the supplies ready for the men," she bargained. "Fifty-fifty."

"You've got a deal."

Time-wise, she'd gotten the better end of the bargain. While he did the warehouse work, she showered, then started putting together the numbers on those bids she needed to submit.

She'd finished doing one takeoff, when she heard a pager beep. Molly glanced from the blueprint to the small black box attached to her belt. The red light wasn't blinking.

Her eyes tracked the sound. Underneath the couch, she saw Brandon's beeper. It mildly irked her to stop what she was doing to take messages for Corral Plumbing, but she hopped down off the high stool at the architect's table and crossed the room.

She picked up the pager, automatically touching the tiny white button and reading the number while storing it for Brandon to take care of later. The number seemed vaguely familiar. Placing the pager on her desk, she discounted its importance.

She returned to the blueprints. To make certain she hadn't pushed the wrong button and erased the number, she jotted it down on her scratch pad. As she wrote the numbers, she had the odd feeling they were ones she'd dialed.

Whose number is it? she wondered. Curiosity got the better of her. Why worry about it?

She called up the data-base files on her computer and entered the number. Her eyes widened when she read the name: Mickey Kasper. He was the lead man on the crew her father had fired right before his accident.

Why would Kasper be paging Brandon?

She asked that question when Brandon came into the office.

"I hired him a couple of weeks ago," Brandon replied matter-of-factly. He clipped the pager to his belt. Thinking out loud, he added, "Kasper must have run short on copper pipe."

"Did you check his references before you hired him?"

"No time. I needed a copper crew so badly I'd have hired Lucifer," he admitted dryly. "Why?"

"John fired that crew. They're the ones who put the wrong grade of pipe in that house I had to re-plumb."

"Guess I'd better tell the riding boss to keep a sharp eye out on them."

"I'd tell him to fire Kasper," Molly blurted. Realizing she was telling Corral whom to hire and fire, she amended, "But I'm not short on copper crews."

"No, you were short on riding bosses. Still are."

Molly closed her eyes and dropped her pencil. "You're going to volunteer, aren't you?"

"Nope. I know better." Brandon grinned at her. "I'm just going to do it."

She opened her eyes, but his smile sanitized the dirty look she planned on giving him. She propped her chin on her hand and sighed. "There's no stopping you, is there?"

"I gave your father my word."

"I know. You've told me. He's told me. But dammit, Corral, I can supervise my own crews."

He gestured toward the rolls of blueprints. "And do the bids. And order the materials. And fix the screwups. And stock the warehouse. And—"

"Stop." Molly raised both hands. "I give up. Go! Do your job and mine, if it makes you happy!"

"Smart decision, Ms. Winsome."

She wanted to be furious with him for that remark, but she couldn't fake it. "Do your riding boss a favor, would you? Call John. Ask him about Kasper."

To placate her, he nodded. "Can I use your phone?"

"Put a quarter in the cash box," she joked. He must have taken her seriously, because he reached in his pocket. "Save your money, Corral. Just let me talk to John when you're finished."

Smiling at her, Brandon dialed the hospital's number.

"Good morning, Kate," he greeted warmly. "Brandon Corral here. How are you?"

"Better now that you've called. Your ears must have been buzzing."

"Why?"

"John and I were discussing the asking price for Winsome Plumbing."

Glad Molly couldn't hear what her mother had said, he pressed the receiver to his ear. He glanced over his shoulder. Molly appeared to be absorbed in what she was doing, but he felt fairly certain she was eavesdropping on his conversation.

"Oh?" he replied noncommittally. "I'm glad to hear John is feeling better."

Kate must have realized he couldn't talk freely. "Is Molly with you?"

"I'm sitting at her desk. She's pretending to be preparing bids."

"I'm not pretending," Molly disclaimed loudly.

"Yes, ma'am." Brandon put his hand over the mouthpiece. "John wants to speak to me privately."

"Trade secrets?"

"I won't know until you leave the room." He paused, listening to Kate. Brandon had the distinct feeling of being squeezed between a rock and a hard place, but he repeated what Kate told him. "John says I'm to drop by the hospital at my convenience if you're being nosy."

In a raised voice, Molly said for her father's ears, "He'll be in the hospital stretched out beside you if you're going to exclude me while you two *men* discuss Winsome Plumbing's business."

Brandon handed her the phone. "I'm an innocent third party."

"Innocent my size elevens." She took the phone. "Hello."

John chuckled. "You aren't going to yell at a crippled man, are you?"

Instantly contrite, she answered softly, "No, I'm not. Thank you for the note, Dad. I was touched."

"You don't think I'm getting to be a sentimental old fool, do you?"

"No. More like the sweetest dad in the whole state of Texas." She knew she was embarrassing him when he started clearing his throat loudly. "How are you, Dad?"

"On the road to rapid recovery. Between you and me?" He chuckled. "I think the nurse panicked and misdiagnosed heartburn for a heart attack."

"The nurses can't be too careful as far as I'm concerned."

"Stop fussing, Molly. I'll be back to work in no time. Why did Corral call here?"

"He hired Kasper's crew."

"Those no-accounts? You better put Corral back on the phone, would you?"

Molly smiled smugly and flipped the receiver to Brandon. "He wants to fill your ear about Kasper.

I'm going to give Yolanda her instructions for the day while he chews—"

"My cute butt," Brandon mouthed, quoting her.

"Exactly."

Brandon waited until she'd left her office to say to John, "Yes, sir?"

"Kate and I have been talkin', reconsidering your offer to buy out my share of Winsome Plumbing."

Brandon waited, feeling the rush of adrenaline he always felt when a new acquisition was being discussed. Now he had a handle on why John had insisted on giving him the password to the computer. John wanted him to have access to all the information he'd need to make a fair offer.

Not a wise business decision on his part, Brandon mused. Automatically his grandfather's bargaining advice came to mind: never pay sticker price and never give the opposition the edge.

He picked up a pencil and sluggishly rotated it from eraser end to the lead, over and over. "And what did the two of you decide?"

"I might be interested in selling out." John nervously laughed. "Of course, you'd have to deal with Molly for her minority share of the stock."

At this point in the negotiation, he usually asked the seller to name a price. But this wasn't any seller. Aside from how he felt about Molly, the bond forged between John and him the night of the accident made these negotiations completely different.

"Molly won't sell," Brandon said succinctly.

"She might if he made the right offer," Brandon heard Kate say to John.

"Hush, Kate. Molly isn't for sale. Whatever we decide, Brandon and Molly will have to make their own decisions." To Brandon, he said, "I won't sell the company out from under her, though. You understand that, don't you?"

"I do."

"In that case, why don't you think about what you can afford and get back to me. Okay?"

Brandon rotated the pencil faster, knowing he should coerce John into stating a sticker price. Business is business, his mind clamored, but he replied aloud, "Fine, John. There's no rush."

"Tell Molly not to work too hard." John chuckled. "She's parent-deaf and won't hear what I tell her. But she might listen to you."

"I'll tell her. You take care of yourself and get well. I'll talk to you soon. Bye."

As he hung up the phone, he dropped the pencil he'd paced himself with into Molly's middle desk drawer. John had expected an offer, and rightly so. A couple of weeks ago he would have made one and been glad to have eliminated another competitor.

He stared at the map on the wall. The flags could be one color—blue. There would be no line of demarcation between north and south Austin. John could be sitting in a bass boat, while he sat in the driver's seat at Corral Plumbing.

Skip the coulda-wouldas, he chastised himself. You blew it. You had him in the palm of your hand. Instead of squeezing your fingers, you dropped the ball.

"You look glum," Molly said, entering her office. She hoped Brandon would volunteer the reason behind Kate's asking to speak to him with her out of the office. When he kept silent, she prodded, "I told you Dad thought Kasper's crew did terrible work."

Brandon closed the center drawer. As he rose from behind her desk, he said, "I think you'd better sit down, Molly."

"Don't get up," she said with an impish grin.

The picture of her on his lap when he broke the news wasn't a pleasant sight. Distance would provide a safety factor he might need. He held the chair and waited for her to be seated.

"John wants to sell Winsome Plumbing," he stated baldly, unable to think of a gentle way to lower the boom. "He wants to sell and I want to buy."

Molly was stunned. She plopped into her chair. "It's his heart problem, isn't it?"

"He didn't say. I didn't ask."

"I wish he'd consulted with me first. It's not like you're—" She clamped her hand over her runaway mouth.

"Family?"

Brandon picked up the framed picture of John and Molly on the desk. As he studied the closeness between the two, the old feeling of being on the outside looking in swamped him. He couldn't superimpose his image between them. There wasn't room for him in this picture.

"I didn't mean to exclude you, Brandon." The stark expression on his face made her want to stuff what she'd said back in her mouth. "No more than Dad meant to leave me out in the cold."

"John said I'd have to negotiate with you for your shares in the company." He returned the photograph to its rightful place. "How much, Molly? What do you want?"

Hurt that he dared to put a price tag on what she considered to be her identity, she blurted an astronomical figure.

Without missing a heartbeat, Brandon cupped the side of her face in his hand. "Does that include the cost of your move?"

"Move?"

"To the lake house, to live with me."

He had to be kidding. She searched his eyes, uncertain he wasn't making fun of her. His pupils had expanded, and were large enough to reflect her troubled face. "You'd pay that?"

"Twice over."

Both flattered and appalled, she caught his wrist. She hesitated, not knowing whether to fling it from her or hold on for dear life. "For what?"

"Family." His eyes burned with fierce desire. "Children. At least two." To block any loopholes in his offer, he added dryly, "Naturally, I'd expect to be the father."

Molly shook her head in astonished disbelief. His offer would have held great appeal if he'd thrown in love, marriage and eternal commitment as fringe benefits. After last night, he should have known that his money and motherhood weren't what she saw in her imaginary crystal ball for her future.

Before she could adamantly refuse, Brandon severed eye contact and ambled to the door. "I'll tell you what I told your father—think it over. I'm in no rush."

The door closed noiselessly behind him. Molly pinched herself to make certain her imagination hadn't played tricks on her.

"Ouch!" She wasn't dreaming. This nightmare was real.

Her eyes moved to the picture he'd stared at. What had Corral seen? Two people, or the warehouse behind where they stood? Was it family or the family business he wanted?

She should have called his bluff, she decided, wondering what he would have done. Called the bank to issue a cashier's check? After he got off the phone, she would have had to call the local mental hospital to book him a room!

Feeling slightly dizzy and disoriented, she folded her arms on the desk and dropped her head on them. One of us is crazy! He for making such an outrageous offer, and she for thinking he was serious.

"Later we'll laugh about this," she whispered, deciding his bizarre offer had more to do with too much hard work and too little sleep than it had to do with reality. "It has to be a joke. Corral knows he can't buy my love."

Why would he?

She was all too willing to give her love to him, free of charge. But she wouldn't sell her shares of Winsome Plumbing to him. Not for any price.

Yolanda came into her office wearing a devilishly sly smile on her face. "You'll never guess who I just got off the phone with."

"Who?" Molly propped her head in her hand. "Lucifer?"

"The secretary at the plumbing inspector's office, Celeste Winston."

"Please, please tell me there aren't any more red stickers stuck on our pipes," Molly begged. "I can't face another day of hunt-and-seek!"

"Those red stickers must be contagious. According to Beverly, Corral Plumbing developed a rash of them yesterday."

"Oh no! Did you tell him?" Molly jumped from the chair and rounded the desk. "He just left my office. I'll see if I can catch him."

"He's gone."

Molly picked up the phone to page him, then slammed it down when she saw his pager on her desk. "I'll call his secretary to get his cellular phone number," she muttered.

"He's gonna be number two, isn't he?"

"Corral isn't interested in becoming a number."

"I'd swear he has the makings of good husband material," Yolanda insisted, watching Molly closely.

"Yes, this is Molly Winsome," she said, identifying herself to the person who'd answered the phone. "I need Mr. Corral's cellular phone number, please." As she listened, she jotted down the number and repeated, "It's on the fritz? Thanks. I'll give it a try. Oh, wait. You wouldn't happen to know what subdivision the Kasper crew is working in, would you?"

Next to the number she wrote Wood Hollow. The pencil's point snapped from pressure. She thanked the receptionist for being helpful, then hung up the phone.

"Kasper's crew is working for Corral?"

Molly nodded. Turning on her monitor, she stroked keys until she was in the data base. "I'm calling Harold."

"What for?"

"I can't go spy on Kasper myself or I would. Harold is the personification of a good ol' boy." She dialed his pager, then punched in her own phone number. "He'll be able to find out what no-good Kasper is up to if anybody can."

Yolanda grinned. "Tell me you haven't fallen in love with Brandon Corral. I won't believe you, but frankly, I don't think you can get that big a lie through your lips."

Family. Two children. I'll expect to be the father.

She could almost hear his offer. Marriage wasn't part of the deal, she reminded herself. Last night he'd said he loved her, but he must have lied. Otherwise he wouldn't have tried to buy her.

Try though she did, her redheaded temper failed to whip up any anger.

"He told me he was married to Corral Plumbing." Molly pulled her hair over her shoulder and began braiding it. "I should have listened, Yolanda."

"Is that a yes, you do?"

"Yes. I love him."

"Don't listen to that I'm-a-confirmed-bachelor bull-roar. I'm on number five and that's what they all said." Yolanda perched on the desk and leaned toward Molly. "Want to know the surefire way to trap the elusive male?"

"How?"

"Spices," Yolanda confided in a whisper. "Nutmeg, cinnamon, ginger..."

Certain Yolanda was pulling her leg, she inquired, "Do I eat them, feed them to him, or rub them on my body?"

"You invite him to your house while you're baking the spices in a fruitcake."

Now she felt certain Yolanda was kidding her. "Men hate fruitcake."

Yolanda's dark Spanish eyes gleamed wickedly as she expressively shrugged one shoulder. "It worked for me. There must be a reason the top layer of a traditional wedding cake is always a fruitcake."

The telephone rang. "That's Harold."

"I'll type my recipe into your computer," Yolanda offered with persistence.

By noon, Molly was cruising through the subdivision where her crews worked. She'd baited the trap for Kasper's men and checked on her own crews. Pleased with their progress, she couldn't understand why a gnawing feeling of apprehension tightened the muscles in her neck.

Corral would be too busy fixing Kasper's screwups to get to the hospital. By the time he did, she would have convinced her father to reconsider selling his half of Winsome Plumbing. She could manage the company, with or without John's help. Wasn't she proving that?

"One day without a major disaster," she muttered dryly. "Not a profound success story."

She massaged her neck and grimaced. Maybe she hadn't proven herself yet, but she could. She would.

She drew a deep, ragged breath and exhaled slowly. If she could take care of her business *and* solve Corral's vandalism problem, both men would back off, wouldn't they?

Chapter Twelve

"Thank God you came back to the office!" Mrs. O'Connor exclaimed, bustling along behind Brandon as he strode through to his office. Her short legs were no match for his long stride. "There's a problem at Wood Hollow."

"Red stickers." There was no point explaining what the problem had been. Mrs. O'Connor had worked for him for years, but she still didn't know the difference between a bowl wax and a pipe collar. "I took care of them."

She poked her wire-framed glasses to the bridge of her nose, a gesture of disapproval, as she glared at her boss's back. He hadn't shaved. His jeans and shirt were streaked with red clay. Damp circles of perspiration stained the underarms of his shirt. He looked like a common laborer.

Brandon glanced over his shoulder and saw Mrs. O'Connor adjust her glasses and sniff. Rather than listen to one of her you're-the-boss-not-a-laborer lectures, he said, "Give me five minutes to clean up, then I'll be with you."

"I called those reinspections in before lunch." She raised her voice in order for Brandon to hear her over the water he ran into the sink. "But I just got off the phone with Mac, for the fifth time in as many minutes."

Brandon splashed his face with water, then lathered it with a cloud of shaving cream. After he shaved, then changed clothes, he was going to the hospital to talk to John. Over dinner, he hoped to convince Molly she wouldn't mind being included as part of a package deal.

Mentally he superimposed Molly's image in the mirror. She'd be riled, but he'd calm her. He loved the way she could be spitting mad one minute and laughing the next.

"Brandon Corral, can you hear me?" Mrs. O'Connor demanded.

"Yeah?" He rinsed the razor, then swiped the razor along his jaw. "Go ahead. What's the problem now?"

"He caught the vandal."

Impossible, he thought, lifting his chin to shave his neck. He'd sent Kasper's crew packing the minute he'd laid eyes on them.

"Harold Somebody-or-other," Mrs. O'Connor yelled. "Mac wants to know what to do with him."

"Call the cops and have him arrested for malicious mischief."

"Are you sure that's what you want done?"

Trepidation detonated in his chest, warning him to move the sharp blade away from his Adam's apple. His entire body tensed. His heart hammered in his chest as he asked, "Why not?"

"He's one of John Winsome's men."

Mrs. O'Connor heard a foul expletive as the razor crashed against the sink bowl. Her boss emerged from the bathroom, scrubbing the foam off his face. A small trickle of blood ran down his neck.

"Go call Mac. Tell him to send Harold home." His voice was thick with hurt and anger and pain. "I'll take care of him, in my own time, my own way."

The fury Mrs. O'Connor heard in Brandon's voice cautioned her not to argue. His upper lip had curled back; he'd snarled like a wild animal who'd been backed into a corner, ready to retaliate.

"Go!" he shouted, a red haze blanketing his vision. "Wait a minute. After you talk to Mac, place a call to Molly Winsome at Winsome Plumbing. Tell her it is imperative for her to come by here after work, *before* she goes to the hospital to see her father."

"Oh. Oh dear, I just remembered." Mrs. O'Connor fanned her flushed cheeks. "John Winsome is in the hospital. Do you suppose it was his daughter who..."

"Get out of here!" Brandon roared, not caring if his secretary went straight into her office and typed up another letter of resignation. "Now!"

Molly's treachery made him feel as though his body was as fragile as a crystal goblet, one about to disintegrate into a million pieces. From his desk he picked up a glass paperweight. Inside it, fake snow swirled around a miniature replica of the Eiffel Tower. His parents had sent it to him last Christmas. He weighed it in his hand.

"Airport trash," he muttered. Mingling the causes of his misery, he hurled the paperweight against the tufted leather sofa across his office. It landed with a dissatisfying thud.

He burrowed the heels of his hands in his eyes to blot out the image of Molly Winsome. Damn her, she'd made him dare to dream of having a family of his own. Her treachery had shattered the dream, and him.

Molly glanced around the receptionist's area, comparing its plushness with the utilitarian starkness of Stephanie's office. Several women looked up from their computer stations to watch her as she proceeded to the desk closest to the front door.

Slightly nervous, she ran her hands down the outside seams of her gray skirt, then adjusted the collar of her crisp, white shirt. Winsome's logo embellished the pocket of her jacket and the trench coat draped across her arm.

"I'm Molly Winsome," she said to the young woman at the desk. "Mrs. O'Connor called. I believe Mr. Corral is expecting me."

Unnervingly, the office became noticeably silent. She could hear the fluorescent lights hum overhead. Her nervousness increased.

She hadn't been surprised when Yolanda had relayed Mrs. O'Connor's message to her. Undoubtedly Brandon was going to retract his outrageous offer. Cockiness covered his embarrassment, as usual;

otherwise he wouldn't have commanded her appearance.

The only thing she regretted was not having heard from Harold. It would have given her untold pleasure to be able to prove Kasper's men were the culprits. Maybe she'd have good news when she paged Harold from the hospital.

"Right this way," the receptionist replied, rising and leading the way through a set of double doors.

Molly followed the petite woman, shortening her stride, being careful her size elevens did not step on the backs of the receptionist's stiletto high heels.

As she strode through the door, she saw Brandon standing at a row of tall windows overlooking the pipe yard. Outside, a forklift moved pallets of white pipe. The driver's jerky movements indicated his desire to get his work finished before the dark gray rain clouds fulfilled their threat of a cloudburst.

"Shut the door, Molly," he commanded softly, not wanting his office staff eavesdropping on their conversation.

"Do you want the lights on?" she asked, noticing his office was becoming increasingly gloomy as the storm approached.

"No."

"It looks as though we're in for another blue norther," she commented, closing the door. Teasing, she added, "Be glad you aren't on a rooftop."

"All hell is going to break loose shortly," he murmured, his voice oddly hoarse. He turned. His arms had been at his sides. Involuntarily they rose, opening to her as though uninformed of her treachery. "Come here and watch it."

Molly crossed the room, fully aware of his dark, penetrating eyes watching her every move. It's the skirt, she mused, smiling. Jeans and slacks were her usual attire. He stared at her knee-length skirt as though he'd never seen a pair of female legs.

She wished she'd worn a pair of high heels, then remembered she'd left them behind in Dallas years ago.

"You don't have to apologize for the indecent offer you made this morning," she said, prepared to forgive him without a hassle. "Impetuosity doesn't suit you or your bank account."

"Is that what it was?" he asked, his voice barely audible.

With her face lifted up, her glorious flaming hair curling over her shoulders, he couldn't resist the temptation to taste his dream one last time. When her lips parted to answer him, he kissed her thoroughly, momentarily triumphing in her surrender as she twined her arms around his neck and hotly returned his kisses.

His leg pushed aside the desk chair as he nudged Molly toward his desk. With his knee between hers, he bodily leaned her across the polished walnut surface. Her jacket fell open, exposing her breasts.

Harshly he ordered, "Tell me about Harold. Tell me why you had him sabotaging my men's work."

"What? I didn't!" she denied, in a state of shock from his mercurial change of mood.

"Harold did this on his own?"

"No! I mean, I didn't send Harold to your job site to tear up the pipe. I sent him to find—"

"Don't lie to me!" He grabbed her shoulders, straightening, pulling her off the desk. "My men caught Harold stomping the plastic test caps down the drainpipes!"

He turned her head so she could see the official papers she'd lain on. Bill of Sale, she read, gasping, feeling his anger as his stronger hands bit into her upper arms. Paid receipts were strewn beside the offensive document. A picture of her and her father had been torn in two.

No! John wouldn't sell out! She didn't know which hurt the most—Brandon believing she was responsible for sabotaging his work or her father betraying her by selling out.

"Please, Brandon, believe me. You know I'd never send Harold over to damage your work."

"I can't hear one lying word that comes from your mouth. But you listen to me and mark my words." Slowly, with cruel deliberation, he said, "I own Winsome Plumbing. You're father signed the papers this afternoon."

"No!" Violently trembling, she said, "You don't. I won't sell you my shares."

"Keep them. They'll be worthless, because I'm the majority stockholder. I'm closing down your shop." He peeled his fingers off her, smiling menacingly down at her. "I'm stealing what you want most... your identity."

"Oh, Brandon, listen to me," she begged. "This is all a mix-up, a horrible mistake. Have you forgotten? My work was damaged, too! You helped fix it!"

He laughed, a cruel, bitter sound. "Very clever ploy. All a part of the hoax. Who'd suspect you were behind this when you were drowning in a sea of red stickers. But your double-crossing plan failed."

"Please, Brandon, don't do this to me, to us. You're making a terrible mistake." She would have pleaded on bended knee, but thank God her pride prevented her knees from sagging to the floor. Although her heart felt as though it was breaking, her eyes remained dry. "Don't you know that I love you?"

"Love? How convenient," he droned sarcastically. "Why don't you write it on a postcard and mail it from the four corners of the earth."

"Damn you, Brandon Corral! Don't you dare compare what I feel for you with your parents' shameful neglect!"

He turned his back on her. Large droplets of water splatted on the windows. "Your lies are wasted on me, Molly. You don't give a damn about me. Why don't you just get the hell out of here and I'll forget you exist?"

Look at me, she beseeched silently. *Can't you see that I'm innocent? I'd never betray you.*

When he did turn toward her, his black eyes appeared dead, emotionless. Molly felt as though she'd become invisible, as though she was so insignificant he could see right through her.

Her shoes seemed weighted with concrete as she crossed his office to the door. She picked her coat up off the chair. With her hand on the doorknob, she glanced over her shoulder, hoping beyond her wildest dreams that he believed her.

She saw his finger on the intercom button and heard "Mrs. O'Connor, will you escort Ms. Winsome off the property?"

He pivoted toward the window. Rivulets of water poured down the huge panes. He knew she'd gone when he heard the door close. Only then did he collapse into his desk chair.

Elbows on his desk, head in his palms, he stared at the torn newspaper picture of Molly and John. The black-and-white picture captured the movement of her hair, the sparkle in her eyes, her womanly figure. Something inside his chest tightened, shriveling, growing hard and impervious.

He didn't need her.

Didn't love her.

He'd have what he wanted: Winsome Plumbing.

Maybe not today, but eventually they'd go broke.

He'd win. Winning was important to him.

Then why did he feel cold all the way to his bone marrow, as though he'd died?

"I didn't do it." In a state of shock, Molly mumbled her claim of innocence as she trudged toward the exit. "I don't know who lied to him, but it wasn't me."

"Put on your raincoat," Mrs. O'Connor entreated, watching the young woman's shoulders shudder. "It's raining. You'll catch cold."

Molly heard Brandon's secretary speaking quietly, but the pain bursting inside her left her deaf and numb. She watched the thin, red streak of lipstick move. It was as though the woman communicated in a foreign language.

"I begged him. Why wouldn't he believe me?" Molly whispered, seeing concern in Mrs. O'Connor's eyes. "He knows I only lie when it's for the other person's good. You believe me, don't you?"

Mrs. O'Connor took the coat and draped it around Molly's slumped shoulders without a reply. Her lips compressed into a straight line of disapproval.

Molly walked through the door Mrs. O'Connor held open for her. Rain fiercely pelted her, stinging her face and hands. She stopped and looked up, unfazed by the torrential downpour.

A person could drown. Molly didn't find the possibility of being caught in a flash flood the least bit dangerous. She felt as though she'd already gone under for the third time.

Automatically she strode toward the parking lot. She'd parked Betsy between two late-model trucks with Corral Plumbing branded on the sides. She had to tug hard twice to get the door open. She took the key chain from her coat pocket, removed the ignition key and placed it on the seat.

Betsy belonged to Brandon.

"Goodbye, love," she murmured, shutting the door.

Back inside the office building, Mrs. O'Connor watched the forlorn figure tramping through the puddles of water as if they didn't exist. She glanced at the paper gliding through the laser printer.

She'd met Molly Winsome only once, under tragic circumstances, but she'd seen the truth shining in those clear, blue eyes. She believed Molly.

Brandon Corral had made the worst mistake of his life.

Mrs. O'Connor removed the paper from the tray and militantly marched toward her boss's office. She'd gone through hell each time his parents jetted in and out of Brandon's life. She could only imagine what the next six months would be like around Corral Plumbing.

Not bothering to knock, she strode into his office. "It's official. I quit."

Before Brandon could lift his head off his arms to offer her a raise, she was gone.

Drenched to the skin, Molly made a wet trail as she left the hospital elevator.

"Miss? Are you okay?" a nurse pushing a cart asked with concern. "You're soaked."

"I'm fine," Molly replied automatically, then bit her lip and corrected the lie with the truth. "I'm wet. Rainwater. I won't melt."

"Here." The nurse stooped down and removed a towel from the bottom shelf of the cart. "You're Kate's daughter, aren't you?"

"Yes." Molly unfolded the towel. She dabbed her face to pacify the nurse. "Thanks."

"You'd better dry your hair, too. You're risking your health when you come into an air-conditioned hospital filled with germs, when you're soaked."

Molly opened her mouth to tell her she'd be okay, but that, too, would be a lie. She swallowed, finding the stranger's kindness a threat to her slender thread of self-control.

"Molly!" Kate hurried down the corridor toward her daughter. "You're drenched. Where have you been? I've called the office, your house."

"I walked."

Kate took the white towel from Molly's trembling hands and briskly toweled the wet skeins of hair cascading down her coat. "Walked? Why? Did Betsy break down?"

"Corral has Betsy," she answered, enduring her mother's ministrations. "He owns her, doesn't he?"

"What did Brandon tell you?" Kate asked, completely baffled.

"Dad sold out," she replied succinctly. She barely noticed that her mother had led her into a vacant lounge. Wearily she sank into a chair. "Didn't he?"

"This reminds me of when you were a little girl." Kate stood beside her daughter and continued to dry Molly's hair. "Rain never bothered you. What was it your father used to say when I fussed at you?"

"'Win Some, Lose Some, Some Get Rained Out,'" Molly supplied, no more eager for her mother to confirm what Brandon had told her than Kate appeared willing to tell.

"Yeah. That's the story of our married life." She used the wet-hair excuse to hold Molly's face against her chest as she dried her hair. Molly didn't squirm and protest the way she had as a little girl. "Winsome Plumbing almost lost some when John fell. Scared me, that's for certain."

"Scared Dad, also?"

"Yeah." Gently Kate pushed the wet, tangled hair off her daughter's wrinkled brow. "I got a note, too. It made me think of what life would be like without him."

"Lonely." Molly nodded.

"Damned lonely. Forty years of marriage down the tube. Made me think of the things we planned to do and never did. Must have had the same effect on John as well. The past couple of days he's been talking about his buddies being up at the lake. And how he's always wanted to have time to plant a garden, maybe raise a few head of stock."

"Retirement?"

"Exactly." Kate folded the towel as she sat in the chair next to Molly. "Brandon made John a good offer."

"Mother, I understand. I don't blame you or Dad."

"Why would you? John knows how you feel about the family business. That's why he changed his mind and turned Corral down flat."

Molly's bent neck snapped up. "What did you say?"

"Yep. Flatter than one of my soggy pancakes. Brandon brought the papers with him to sign, but John told him that Winsome Plumbing was staying where it belonged . . . in your capable hands. Your father didn't sell out."

The Bill of Sale wasn't signed? Corral lied to me? He's the one who perpetrated a hoax!

Why?

Kate smiled at Molly's stunned expression. "Corral did his best to convince John it would be for your own good for him to sell, or at least form a limited partnership."

The slender thread of composure unraveled as Molly sobbed tears of gratitude. Since she'd put the ladder against the house to help Corral off the roof she'd shed more tears than the raindrops in the storm outside. Thank goodness she hadn't wasted any on Corral!

"Corral thinks I ordered Harold to vandalize his buildings," Molly blurted. Humiliated, she grabbed the towel and mopped the tears from her face. "I begged him to believe me, Mom. He...he kicked me out of his office."

Kate bristled. "He kicked you?"

"No," Molly answered truthfully. "He ordered me to leave and said that he never wanted to see or hear from me again." '

"Do you think he used you to try to get the company?"

Several minutes later, John asked the same question after Molly told him what had happened. Shrewdly, seconds later, he added, "Or did Corral think he'd own you if he used his money to buy Winsome Plumbing? The whiz kid is used to buying anything he wants, isn't he?"

Chapter Thirteen

"Mr. Corral." The secretary he'd hired to replace Mrs. O'Connor interrupted him. "Could you slow down and repeat the last sentence, please?"

"Which one?" he asked. "'Sincerely Yours,' or 'Bring it in for me to sign when you've typed it'?"

Flustered, the young woman erased the squiggles she'd made in her shorthand book and smiled vapidly at her boss. "The amount of the bid. Was that five hundred or five thousand?"

"Fifty thousand," he corrected as he strove to maintain his soft-spoken demeanor. Three secretaries in five weeks had dulled his sharp retorts.

"Even?"

"Five-zero-comma-zero-zero-zero," he snapped sarcastically. "Period."

He wanted to undercut Winsome's bid, but with his new secretary's ineptness with numbers, she'd make him a pauper within the year—that is, if she lasted more than a week!

"No cents," she confirmed, her face an indelicate shade of green.

No sense, Brandon agreed with a nod, dismissing her with a wave of his hand. A familiar sinking in the pit of his stomach warned him to put another ad in the paper for an executive secretary.

He swiveled his chair to face the windows. Automatically his gaze skittered over the stacks of pipe to the back corner of the lot. His brow furrowed as he glared at Betsy.

The battered truck was a daily reminder of Molly's treachery. He should have had it towed to the junkyard. Damn her stubborn hide; she should have driven Betsy wherever it was she'd gone.

If ever there was a woman who had enough sense to come in out of the rain, it was his Molly!

Brandon grimaced. She wasn't his.

In fact, the entire local plumbing industry buzzed with her name. She'd changed her bidding strategy. She'd switched from low-profit subdivision homes to high-markup mansions—on his side of Austin.

"And commercial jobs," he muttered, irrationally proud and incensed by her success.

Brandon dragged his eyes from the yellow eyesore. Tomorrow, he vowed silently, he'd call John. He'd been making the same vow daily.

Picking up the receiver, he followed his grandfather's code of not procrastinating. He heard John was supervising the office. He'd call him there.

"John Winsome, please," he requested in a clipped tone. "Brandon Corral calling."

Yolanda rushed into Molly's office to personally notify the new office manager that the long-awaited call had finally arrived. "Corral is on line one."

Adjusting her spectacles, Mrs. O'Connor picked up the receiver and growled, "Have you phoned to apologize?"

"Mrs. O'Connor?" he yelped. No wonder he hadn't been able to contact his ex-secretary to offer her a salary increase! "You're John Winsome's secretary?"

"Office manager. Less pay, mind you, but I've always wanted a title and a small percentage of a business."

Brandon rocked back in his chair, stunned. "Where's John?"

"Toledo Bend."

"He retired?"

"Yes, sir."

"Well, I'll be damned," he declared.

Mrs. O'Connor chirped, "Probably. Broke will suffice nicely. After all, Molly isn't vengeful, like some people I know."

"Vengeful? Me? I could have had Molly's lackey tossed in jail for malicious mischief!"

"You could have, but then we would have had to have charges against you for false arrest, slander and damage to shop. You're the one who ought to be arrested—for criminal negligence! Thanks to you, Molly walked five miles to the hospital in a storm, barefoot, with no umbrella! The way I see it, the very least you owe Molly is an apology."

"Harold was caught with the heel of his boot stuck through a plastic cap at my job site. This was the same type of damage that caused the plumbing inspector to red-tag eight other houses. I don't owe Molly Winsome anything."

"I'm not discussing this with you, Brandon. I know what happened. Obviously you don't."

"Molly lied to you."

"Uh-huh," Mrs. O'Connor droned. "What about the megasized lie you told her? John turned down your offer to buy his half of Winsome Plumbing."

"I got even with her for betraying me," he alleged, justifying his behavior.

"Don't Get Mad, Get Even? That's your grandfather's motto. Why don't you step into the nineties, Brandon? Get in touch with your feminine side. Be intuitive. Compassionate. I really would hate to see you end up a lonely old man like your grandfather."

Family loyalty made Brandon defensive. "He has many friends."

"Business associates, not friends," Mrs. O'Connor modified. "I've known your grandfather since grammar school. I'm here to tell you—he hasn't changed one iota. You'd think he was poor kid from the wrong side of the tracks the way he behaved. Did you know that he used to sell the home-baked pies his mother put in his lunch? I swear, his fingers should have been gnarled by third grade because he'd trade his new pencil for pencil stubs and pennies."

Her bellicose tone changed to one of concern. "If not for your grandmother, bless her soul, your father would have been sent to school dressed like a ragpicker. Within a week after her funeral, your fa-

ther took the money he'd inherited from her and departed." She paused and drew in a deep breath.
"Why don't you stop blaming your father for desert-
ing you long enough to ask yourself why your parents flitted from one sunny climate to another? My
theory is they needed to thaw out. You do, too, before you permanently freeze Molly from your life."

"She . . . betrayed . . . me." He deliberately paused
between each word for emphasis.

Mrs. O'Connor sighed. "Talk to Harold. Then use
some of your hard-earned money to buy yourself
some knee pads. You'll need them when you come
groveling to Molly."

She hung up before Brandon could tell her he'd
never forgive Molly. Betrayal was worse than his parents' desertion. He'd loved her!

Brandon closed his eyes to shut out the pain and
fury Mrs. O'Connor's revelations caused him. Nothing she'd told him about his grandfather surprised
him. Jake Corral loved money; parting with it was his
means of expressing love.

What infuriated him was Molly walking five miles
in a lightning storm! A clear image of her short skirt,
cotton shirt and flimsy shoes increased his anger.

*I'm innocent. Don't do this to me, to us. Don't you
know that I love you?*

He blinked to dispel the image of her gazing up at
him, begging him to trust her. Hell, he knew she was
in financial straits. Hadn't he offered her twice the
value of Winsome Plumbing? He might have for-
given her if she had admitted she'd ordered his job
sites vandalized. She could have told him she was
afraid of losing her customers to him. Or she could

have tossed her hair over her shoulder, lifted her chin defiantly and said, "Gotcha!" Then he might have been able to separate business from his personal life and told her to forget it.

She'd pulled a dirty trick. So what? They were rival competitors. He would have shown her the fake Bill of Sale, and they would have been even. By nightfall, they would have been at his lake house, in his bed, laughing about the incident.

But she had pleaded innocent; he had found her guilty.

"And condemned myself to solitary confinement," he said, mocking his decision.

Brandon heard the intercom buzz and pushed the button. "Yes?"

"The letter you dictated is ready for your signature. Shall I bring it in to your office?"

"No. I'll stop by your desk on my way out."

Not waiting for her to ask him where he was going, Brandon slowly rose from his chair. He pulled open his center desk drawer and removed the key to the yellow truck. He dragged the dull, serrated edge across his thumb, felt no pain, then purposely strode from his office.

Twenty minutes later, Betsy gave up the ghost two blocks south of Apex Supply Company. She'd warned him. Her engine had died twice before making a horrendous clatter and refusing to start.

Unexplainably, Brandon had become emotionally attached to the yellow wreck. As he shut Betsy's hood, he felt as though he'd lost his last friend.

"Ridiculous," he muttered, irked by his sentimentality. He'd owned dozens of vehicles and never formed an attachment to any of them. Unlike his grandfather, he considered a vehicle purely a means of transportation.

But none of them had had a name, or a personality, or belonged to Molly Winsome.

He shoved his hands into his pockets and started walking toward the supply house. From there he'd call a tow truck and a taxi. His snap decision to take Betsy home was foolishness on his part.

Did he think Molly would be so thrilled to see Betsy that she'd—

Brandon squelched the thought before he dared to dream the impossible. Molly had betrayed him. He'd offered her everything and thrown himself in as part of the bargain, and she'd rejected him by attempting to discredit his company.

A cowbell clanged noisily as he opened the door to the supply house. Several men who stood at the counter turned, glanced at him, then went back to placing their orders.

"How you doin'?" one of the clerks cordially greeted, stepping over to wait on him.

"Fine, thanks. Can I use your phone?"

"Sure." The clerk reached under the counter and retrieved the phone. "Help yourself."

Brandon dialed the Corral Lincoln dealership, spoke briefly to the head mechanic, then called a cab company.

"Having truck trouble?" the man standing beside him inquired.

"Yeah." Brandon noticed the Winsome Plumbing logo on the stranger's shirt. Neatly stitched above the front pocket he read the man's name: Harold.

"I'm finished for the day. I could give you a ride. Where are you going?" Harold asked, shifting the toothpick in his mouth to the corner.

Before he could answer, the clerk said, "Are you finished using the phone, Mr. Corral?"

"Yes." He watched Harold puff up like a toad. His chest expanded; he hiked up his jeans and glared without blinking. "We need to talk."

"I got nothin' polite to say to you," Harold spit.

The irony struck Brandon as ludicrous. Harold vandalized his work and he was the bad guy?

"I could have filed charges against you," Brandon reminded him in a low voice filled with menace.

"For what?"

"Checking out the size of my pipe with the heel of your boot?"

Harold bellied up to Brandon, ready to settle their disagreement with his fists. "I was doing you a favor, whiz kid. For a man with a reputation for being smart, you were dumber than a pet rock that day."

"How so?"

"You had Mac run me off without listening to what I had to say first." He rolled the toothpick across his lips, then snapped it in two with his front teeth. He stashed the pieces in his front shirt pocket. "I know who vandalized your work, how and why."

Brandon had the distinct feeling Harold was going to leave him in the dark when the shorter man picked up a handful of fittings off the counter and stowed them in his pants pocket. The pink receipt went in the same pocket as the toothpick.

"I'm listening," Brandon growled with menace.

Stroking the stubble of whiskers on his chin with his knuckles, Harold shook his head. "I don't seem to be able to recall . . ."

"How much?"

Brandon didn't realize he'd insulted the man until he felt Harold's quick jab to his solar plexus. Air whooshed from between his lips, but he managed to remain upright.

"That's for Ms. Molly," Harold wheezed angrily. "You couldn't buy her, either, could you? Why don't you take your worthless money and shove it?"

Clutching Harold by the front of his shirt, Brandon lifted the smaller man off his feet. From behind, two men grabbed his arms and yanked him backward. It was the only thing that saved Harold from having the information bodily shaken out of him.

"Take it easy, Corral," the man holding his right arm grunted, back-stepping until the two men were separated. "Everybody in Austin but you knows Kasper was up to no good. He was being paid by a plumbing contractor out of Dallas."

Brandon's knees buckled. Dark spots swam in front of his face. His strong self-control prevented him from passing out. He held on to the counter until he could walk without stumbling.

As he strode to the truck one thought haunted him: Molly had told him the truth.

Chapter Fourteen

A canopy of green leaves shaded the narrow road leading to the banks of Toledo Bend Lake. Aided by the hand-drawn map Mrs. O'Connor had faxed to him on the sly, Brandon knew exactly where John and Kate had bought their cabin.

Betsy's engine idled softly as he stopped beside a cabin built with hewed oak logs. A wide porch wrapped around the front of the modest home that faced the lake. John and Kate must have been sitting in the porch swing, enjoying the view of the water and the cool autumn breeze, when they saw their truck driving up the lane.

As Brandon turned off the engine, Kate steadied the swing while John levered himself and his bulky cast until he stood upright. Brandon would have liked to see a smile of recognition on John's face. The animosity he did see made his heart sink to his boots.

"It's about time you returned Betsy," John castigated. He put his hand on Kate's shoulder to keep her seated. "What did you do to her?"

"Tune-up." Brandon fondly stroked Betsy's hood. "Had the dents removed and gave her a new paint job." He ambled up the stone path bordered with a wild profusion of asters. "Is Molly here?"

"Yep, she got the message you sent her on the pager," John replied, shifting his weight until he leaned against the log wall. "In case you didn't notice, she didn't return your call."

"She doesn't want to see you," Kate added softly.

Brandon pointed to the bed of the truck. "I brought knee pads."

Kate smothered a giggle with her hand and looked up at John. "Mrs. O'Connor said she told him to grovel."

"You could crawl on your belly and Molly still wouldn't forgive you," John forewarned.

"There's also a tent in the back of the truck," Brandon said with determination. "I'm not leaving until I do see her."

"John." Kate spoke softly, taking his hand and looking up at her husband of forty years. "We wouldn't be here if it wasn't for Brandon. He did save your life. And—"

"Shhh, Kate. This isn't between us and him. You heard what I told Molly."

Kate raised an eyebrow. "That Lone Wolf would never forsake his woman? Or that the writer planned on writing a sequel you wanted to read?" She lifted one shoulder. "Molly didn't know what you meant any more than I did."

John's harsh expression changed as he looked at Brandon. "You do, don't you?"

Grinning, Brandon took the steps to the porch in two bounds. Molly was his woman; he'd never forsake her.

To Kate's total amazement, he crossed to John and gave her husband a back-slapping hug. There was moisture in her eyes when Brandon released John and bent to give her a kiss on the cheek.

While Brandon strode to the screened door, Kate moved beside John. Hope lit both their faces as they squeezed each other's hands.

Brandon crossed the threshold, quietly closing the screen. He could hear water running in the kitchen sink and dishes rattling together. A spicy aroma filled the cabin. Her mother might be a microwave artist, but whatever Molly had in the oven smelled heavenly.

"I'll fix some iced tea and bring it out when I've finished the lunch dishes, Mom," Molly called, not turning from her chore at the sink.

"Let me fix it," Brandon offered, meaning far more than preparing a cold drink. She looked exquisite, wearing shorts and no shoes, her hair cascading down her back. "At least let me try."

Molly whirled around. Iridescent soapsuds dribbled from her hands, unnoticed. She gazed steadfastly at the tall, handsome man a few steps away from her. Instead of his usual cocky smile, lines of stress bracketed his lips as he earnestly studied her.

He'd changed; she had not.

She was still the same dry-eyed woman who'd lowered her pride and begged him to believe her, to trust her. He'd cast aside the love she'd offered and done the unforgivable by callously lying to her.

Mortified, she saw her bare toes curl as his gaze dropped to the floor. And she was angry, damned mad that he'd charmed his way past the sentry she'd posted to keep him away from her. Her parents should have given him the boot!

"Get the hell out of here, Corral!" she blasted, whirling back to the sink and submerging her arms up to her elbows.

"I can't," he replied in an achingly sad voice. "I'm stranded. No wheels."

She felt him narrow the gap between them. Her hands trembled with fury as she tried to grab hold of a slippery plate to throw at him. She wanted to hurt him physically for the pain he'd caused her.

"Don't you dare touch me or I'll scream," she warned. "You smooth-talked your way around my parents, but whatever you said to them won't work with me."

Brandon retreated a step. "Molly, please . . ."

"Please?" she repeated derisively. Fire burned in her eyes as she glanced over her shoulder at him. She wiped her hands on a dish towel. "You've learned that word? You didn't know it the night I saved your hide on a roof. You didn't know it when I used it to beg you to believe me!"

"I'm sorry, so damned sorry," he whispered hoarsely.

Once, what seemed to her like aeons ago, he'd told her never to use that word, either. Agitated, she twisted the damp terry cloth as she fervently wished she could block that memory, along with the other memories that had caused her sleepless nights and days filled with torment.

She dodged around him, needing to put some distance between them. God help you if you try to stop me!

He did. Anticipating her desire to flee to the safety of her parents' arms, he bodily blocked her escape route. He caught her arms before she could land blows that would make Harold's blow to the gut seem like a love tap.

Molly twisted, turned, elbows flying, her bare feet trampling his shoes.

"Stop it, Molly." It required all his strength to restrain her without causing her harm. "You'll hurt yourself."

Her head snapped upward, clipping him on the chin accidentally. She heard him gasp, then felt his arms wrap around her like steel bands around lumber. She couldn't move, other than to do the ultimate damage by bringing her knee into his crotch. She couldn't do that, either, not even to the man who'd broken her heart and thrown her out into the rain.

His large hands began to move beneath her hair, soothing the taut muscles in her back. She held her spine uncompromisingly stiff, but the old magic of feeling his strong, muscular body was spinning a dangerous spell. Unless she could break it, she'd be hopelessly lost.

"Leave," she entreated in a quiet, solemn voice.

"I can't," he murmured against her hair. "I can't function without my heart and soul, Molly. It's wherever you are."

"Don't," she protested weakly. Her hands trembled as she pushed against his chest. "Don't lie."

"I have to say it. It's the truth, the whole truth."

"Truth?" She shuddered. "Here's the truth, Brandon. I've never begged for anything in my life. Never! But I begged you to listen to me. I sent Harold to find out who was sabotaging both our jobs." Warily she glanced up at him. "Your foreman found Harold right after he'd chased one of Kasper's men out of the house that your men had just finished topping out. Nobody would listen to him, either."

"You didn't know what had happened when you came to my office, did you?"

"No." She sighed heavily. "Why didn't you trust me, Brandon?"

"It wasn't you I didn't trust. The bare-boned truth is that somewhere in the darkest part of my mind I still believed I was unlovable. Call it self-preservation or a self-fulfilling prophecy. Whatever. I couldn't allow myself to believe you loved me, because I knew you'd leave me."

"I wouldn't have."

His hold on her changed to a hug. "What I did was wrong, Molly. I was an unfeeling money-making machine until you and your family came into my life." His fingers touched the vulnerable place just beneath her ears as his thumbs raised her chin until their eyes met. "You all breathed life into me, made me think with my heart and feel with my soul. I love you, Molly Winsome. I can prove it."

The tears she shed only in moments of great joy gathered in the back of her throat. "You don't have to prove anything to me, Brandon. I just want to be loved for who I am. Don't expect me to change. Not the way I look, walk, talk or dress."

He wrapped a ringlet of flame-colored hair around his finger. "Only a fool would want to change red hair that looks like it's on fire when the sunlight hits it. And I happen to be particularly fond of those long, gorgeous legs that match my stride. I don't feel as if I'm on a choker chain when I walk with you, sweetheart. No waiting or mincing my steps."

While he spoke, she was unbelievably still. She seemed to be absorbing what he said through every pore in her skin.

"And I can't imagine anyone wanting to change your Southern drawl. Or your wit. Without them you'd be a beautiful mannequin. Empty-headed. One thing is for certain, you're never boring. I've learned to expect the unexpected.

"Most of all," he whispered. "I love how you love, wholeheartedly, without reservation. The way your eyes light up when you see me is like...I don't know, like feeling sunshine on my face on a wintry day."

He took a deep breath before he bared his soul. "I need your warmth, Molly. I've been emotionally frozen most of my life."

Hesitantly she wound her arms around his waist. "And marriage. I want what my parents have. You left that out of your first offer. I won't just move in with you."

His lips curved into a smile as he kissed her forehead. "I'll buy you the biggest, most dazzling diamond engagement ring in Texas!"

"No!" She hushed him by brushing her lips against his mouth. "You don't have to buy me anything. I'm yours free, unconditionally. You can be flat broke and I'll love you."

Overwhelmed by emotions, Brandon closed his eyes and kissed Molly, taking full possession of her mouth with a fierce, compulsive need. All his dreams were about her. All he'd seen, heard, touched, smelled and tasted were of Molly. His Molly.

"You have to marry me," he agreed, when their kisses were just short of taking them beyond what John and Kate would have considered acceptable behavior. "I have a rash of red stickers on all my jobs. Mrs. O'Connor's filing system hasn't been cracked by a dozen new secretaries."

Molly laughed, hugging him tighter. "What you need is a crystal ball," she teased, slipping her arm around his waist and leading him into the living room. Pointing to the low table in front of the sofa, she said, "Like that one?"

"You really do have a crystal ball?"

"Of sorts," she replied, grinning at him as he sat beside her on the sofa. "Take a look."

Brandon carefully lifted the ball in both hands and peered into it. He saw a drawing of a house, a man beside a woman with flaming red hair, two children and a battered yellow pickup truck parked beside a new truck. Looking closer, on each truck he saw a WWW brand, with a pipe fence around the lettering.

"No more 'Win Some, Lose Some, Some Get Rained Out,'" she explained softly, her love shining in her eyes. "It's 'Win-Win-Win,' with a Corral fence."

"A partnership," he agreed, returning her smile as he remembered the bet they'd made. "I keep my belt and you keep your boots?"

Later he'd show her the Bill of Sale he had the lawyers make out to her, he mused contentedly, folding her into his arms.

Much later, she thought, she'd thank Yolanda for her fruitcake recipe. She'd freeze the cake in the oven and save it for the top layer of their wedding cake.

For now, they'd be too busy making plans for the future—one that would last through eternity.

* * * * *

Silhouette®

Bestselling Author

MAGGIE SHAYNE

Continues the twelve-book series—FORTUNE'S CHILDREN—
in **January 1997** with Book Seven

A HUSBAND IN TIME

Jane Fortune was wary of the stranger with amnesia who
came to her—seemingly out of nowhere. She couldn't deny
the passion between them, but there was something
mysterious—almost dangerous—about this compelling
man...and Jane knew she'd better watch her step....

MEET THE FORTUNES—a family whose legacy is greater than
riches. Because where there's a will...there's a *wedding!*

Look us up on-line at: http://www.romance.net

FC-7